Enjoy the romance!

Mary Dean

BE MY
Valentine

ANTHOLOGY

Caleb Pine ~ Charlene Johnson ~ D. S. Tossell ~
Katie Holland ~ Lisa Colodny ~ Mary Dean ~
McKenzie Stark ~ Shawna Hunter ~ Will Hallewell

Copyright

Editing by KP Editorial Services
Formatting & Cover Design by KP Designs
- www.kpdesignshop.com
Published by Kingston Publishing Company
- www.kingstonpublishing.com

Table of Contents

Fighting for Love

A Punching Down the Walls

Short Story

by

Caleb Pine

Chapter 1

Ash

"You like that?" I asked Diego, as I dragged my tongue down his muscular torso. I tried not to be distracted by the sinful sounds that were coming out of his mouth. I looked up at Diego as his eyes were closed. I still was stunned that this hot guy was still attracted to me. His sleeve of tattoos on his arms and left leg popped on his tan skin. His dark hair was grown out, and he was rocking a beard. I had to admit that I found him more attractive now than when I first met him. Maybe, it was because we were happily in love.

Diego lifted his head and gave me a grown. I knew he was sexually frustrated, and he wanted to get off. His pre-cum was all over my hands. He couldn't do anything about it because his hands were tied to the bedpost. I had told him how I want to spice things up in the bedroom, and the answer was bondage. He couldn't vocalize anything because he has a gag in his mouth.

Diego always liked being in control, but today, he was my slave. I bent down and dragged my tongue over the tip of his cock. He let out a groan and a soft whimper. "Someone seems to be liking that," I said, as he nodded his head. "Does someone want to get off?" I asked, toying with him.

He looked at me and glared at me. He let out a filthy snarl. I bent down and engulfed Diego's massive cock inside me. There was nothing petite or small about Diego. Especially, now that he was on a stride of boxing matches, he had bulked up more, which was a benefit to me more than anything.

I bobbed my head up and down his cock dragging my tongue up his shaft. I could taste the sweetness of Diego's come coating the roof of my mouth. His cock was throbbing in my mouth, and I knew he was about to explode.

I went faster with my motions. I heard all the whimpers and groans coming out of his mouth until finally he unloaded into my mouth with a giant muffled grunt coming out of him. I took every last drop of him before I decided that I was done with him.

I pulled his cock out of his mouth, and I walked over to take the gag out of his. He was breathing heavily, and he looked at me with such amazement. "I will never know why anyone would let go of you. That was the hottest thing I have ever experienced," he said.

I shrugged. "I do what I can." I leaned down and kissed him on the lips. The butterflies would never go away. Six months ago, I would have never guessed that this where both of us would have belonged. It had been hard after his suicide attempt, but we were in a better place. He had gotten rid of his guilt for Vanessa, and I was able to finally be in a happy relationship with someone.

He cleared his throat, which caused me to break out of my trance. I looked at him. "Yes?"

He began shaking his arms. "Do you mind untying me? I have to use the bathroom," he informed me.

"Oh shit! Sorry." I began to untie his arms. He got off the bed and ran to the bathroom. When he came out of the bathroom, he walked over and began kissing my neck. I felt his tongue and teeth on me. "You know I find it sexy when you take control like that," he said.

I felt myself getting aroused. I grabbed a fistful of his newly long hair and pulled his head towards my lips. The kiss was filthy, and I loved every second of it. We began kissing each other, and he deepened the kiss. I let out a groan, and I wanted to get release.

He slid his hands down my body, and I knew it was my turn to get off. We would have gone further if my phone hadn't gone off. We both let out a disgruntled grunt. I went to grab my phone. I saw it was Edgar. I picked it up right away. "Is everything alright?" I asked.

"Yeah, it's all good. Do you mind picking up my shift in the morning?" He asked.

I rolled my eyes. "You're getting laid tonight, aren't you?"

"Sorry, we all couldn't find our prince charming at a boxing ring."

"Technically, I found him at a bar," I argued.

"Regardless, can you pick up my shift?" he asked.

"Yeah, fine," I said.

"Thanks so much," he said, before he hung up.

I got off the bed. "Sorry, I need to go back to my place to grab a work shirt for tomorrow."

I turned to see the frown on his face. "Do you really need to cover his shift?" he asked.

I leaned forward. "Yes, since he's covering my shift so we can celebrate our first Valentine's day together." I didn't know why I was looking forward to this year. Usually it was a disaster with Tristian that led to me getting beaten because it wasn't up to his standards.

"Are you going to come back?" he asked.

I walked over to put my shoes on. "Probably not since it's an early shift."

He let out a little whine. I thought it was adorable. He was someone that you didn't want to find yourself alone with in an alley, but he was a giant teddy bear. "So, I'm not going to, have anyone to cuddle with tonight?"

"Well if you made room for me in your drawer, then I would stay over," I said. I grabbed my phone off the nightstand. "I don't get why you still have so much of Vanessa's clothing. I thought her parents grabbed all of her stuff," I said. I didn't realize what I was saying until it came out of my mouth.

I turned to Diego. I saw how stiff he was on the bed. He went back behind his walls, and I knew it was because of all the guilt he had from her death. Even six months later, it still fucked with him. I didn't want to tell him how much it bothered me. We have been going solid for six months, but he was still holding on to her. We couldn't full be a couple until he let go of her and his guilt surrounding her death.

He turned to me. "I'm sorry." There were tears in his eyes.

I shook my head. "It's not your fault at all." I leaned down and kissed him on the lips. I hoped that was enough reassurance to get him to not go down the rabbit hole. "Why don't I get an Uber, and I'll be back in twenty minutes?" I suggested.

He gave me a weak smile. "I'll pay for the Uber," he offered.

"Deal," I said, giving him a big smile trying to smooth it over.

I walked out of the bedroom to the living room to see right in front of me a photo of Vanessa and Diego still hanging out. I wanted to not be jealous of a dead girl, but I wasn't anywhere in this apartment. I knew he had built a life with her, but what about the life he was trying to build with me?

Chapter 2

Diego

I woke up the next morning with Ash in my arms. It was kind of funny how massive my frame was to his lean frame. It was a feeling that I never wanted to go away. I could tell when he came back last night, that he was bothered that he couldn't have a drawer. I slowly got out of bed, and I let him sleep in. He had another hour until he needed to get up for work.

I couldn't stop thinking about the sadness in his hazel eyes last night. I wanted nothing more than to run my fingers through his light brown hair, and tell him that I loved him more than anyone else. His happiness meant more to me than my own.

I threw on some gray joggers and a black hoodie. I opened the drawer to grab socks and closed it. I looked down at the bottom drawer. I knew that drawer very well. It was clothes that Vanessa couldn't get rid of. It was the last of the items her parents didn't take. All I had to do was give it to good will, and then we wouldn't be having this odd tension between us.

I sighed because I knew what the simple answer was, but I didn't know how to execute it. I was grateful that Ash understood that about me, but it didn't mean that he was going to put up with this forever.

I drove to the gym with my mind only thinking about Ash. I wanted to make this man happy. I wanted him to know that I loved him, but I was so god damn broken. Even after he saved me from pulling the bullet in my head. I've had these thoughts about maybe I should have done it.

I heard those pleas in his broken voice telling me he loved me. I couldn't do that to him. I had done so many selfish things to get where I was in life, and it was the one move that I couldn't accomplish. I wasn't going to break Ash's heart like that. That would be a guilt even worse than my mother's death.

"Earth to Diego," Bobby said, breaking me out of my trance.

I blinked a couple of times, and I looked at him. I was so lost in my own thoughts that I hadn't realize I was punching a punching bag. I looked down, and I had changed into my black gym shorts, white compression tights, and a gray tank top. Sweat was dripping down my body.

"Sorry, I guess I let the day get away from me," I admitted.

Bobby had cut off all of his hair to rock a buzz cut. He was still smaller than me, but he was starting to get a belly. He glared at me. "I'm sorry that I'm trying to train you for your next fight. You know the one to keep your winning streak alive," he said.

I looked at him in disbelief. "I don't know if winning two matches in a row counts as a winning streak," I argued. Yeah, I had beaten my last two competitors, and it shut up the commentators thinking I was a joke. I knew it was because my headspace was better. Ash made me a better fighter and human.

"Do you want to tell me what's going on?" he asked.

I took my gloves. "It's nothing that you need to worry about," I replied.

He nodded. "The Diego wall. How I don't miss those days."

I walked over and grabbed my water bottle. "I'm just going through a lot right now. Ash wants me to give him some stupid drawer, but I can't get the courage to throw away the last of Vanessa's stuff."

"It's been six months," he said softly.

"I know. I'm over Vanessa, but I can't seem to make it official. The apartment is the last thing holding me to her," I admitted. I knew it was so dumb, but I really did love Vanessa. We might have been a disaster together, but she still had my heart for some time.

He walked over and placed a hand on my shoulder. "You need to stop letting the past hold you back. I get that you still blame yourself for her death, but you're in a good relationship. You're the best version of yourself."

"And Vanessa's six feet in the ground," I snapped at him. "How is that fair for her?" I asked. "I'm able to hold the person that I love. I'm able to spend every second of my day knowing that I found my person. She doesn't get that. It's not right."

"But you holding to her stuff, and it's not right to Ash," he said. He walked away leaving me with my thoughts.

I walked into the locker room. I turned on the shower, and I let the hot water calm my emotions. I closed my eyes, and I tried my hardest to forget all about Vanessa and Ash for a second. I just felt like there was once again a war in my head, and I didn't know if I would survive it this time.

I got out of the shower and wrapped the towel around my waist. I almost screamed when I saw Vanessa standing there in a floral dress. Her long black hair was pulled into a ponytail. "You know Bobby is right. You should be moving on from me," she stated.

I groaned and rolled my eyes. "You're going to fight me now, too. Shouldn't you be telling me that you hope I'm miserable till the day I die?" I asked.

"You call me the dramatic one," she commented. "We would never have worked together. You know this. You need to give your all to Ash before it's too late," she said.

"I'm scared," I admitted. I gave my all to Vanessa, and it didn't work out. I didn't want the same for Ash. Vanessa, I knew would be able to walk away from our relationship. I didn't think Ash would be able to walk away so easily, and neither could I with my love for Ash.

Chapter 3

Ash

I was frozen surrounded by stupid Valentine's day cards and candy. I didn't want to believe what I was seeing in front of me. I knew that eventually he would move on, and I had done the same thing. I had left him for someone else, but I thought he would take time get his shit together.

Tristian was currently holding hands with a younger guy, medium build, tall, dark skinned, and a buzz cut. I saw the warmness in Tristian's eyes, and I saw how stupidly in love the guy was for Tristian. I remembered exactly those days where I believed Tristian was going to save me from it all.

I watched as Tristian kiss the guy on the cheek as they checked out their groceries. I spent paid for my groceries and booked it out of the grocery store and parking lot. I didn't know why I felt like my whole world has shattered. I was being so damn naïve to believe that I would never see him again.

I got to Diego's apartment to start the dinner. I tried to get all of the thoughts of Tristian out of my mind, but I then looked at a photo of Vanessa and Diego on the wall. It brought me back to all the words that Wes said to me. I was just another twink he was fucking.

I walked over and grabbed the picture off the wall. I heard the door open. I turned to see Diego walking in. He looked at me confused. "Are you okay?" he asked.

I didn't know why I was filled with so much rage in that moment. I could just hear Wes's laugh in my head. I can just see him and Vanessa laughing telling me that of course Diego didn't love me. Tristian didn't even fight for me back. He just shrugged his shoulders and found someone else. I'm just a warm body to Diego, or he would have gotten rid of all of Vanessa's stuff by now.

I looked into Diego's beautiful eyes, and I knew that I would never be enough for him. I was nothing to him. He told me all those pretty words to trap me just like Tristan did, and what he was doing to his new victim. "You don't love me," I said.

Diego looked confused. "What are you talking about?" he asked, dropping his gym bag off.

I showed him the picture of him and Vanessa. "Why do you still have this hung up?"

"Ash, you know it's because Vanessa passed away."

I shook my head. "It's all lies. You're still in love with her."

"I was leaving her for you," he said. He started walking towards me. "I chose you over her, don't you remember?"

"No, you only chose me because I was your excuse to come out. I mean nothing to you."

I could see the confusion in Diego's eyes. "What are you even talking about? Ash, this isn't you."

"Why don't you have any photos of me around the god damn apartment. Why can't you give me a god damn drawer in your dresser?"

He opened his mouth, but nothing came out. "You have to use your fucking words, Diego," I said. I knew that Diego was hard with his worlds. It was something we had been working on for months, but I was so destroyed right now. I needed him to try because I was an emotional mess.

I honestly thought everything from six months ago was out of my head, but the demons like to show their ugliness whenever they wanted to. It killed me that I gave Diego my lifeline to keep me strong. I was supposed to be strong on my own, and I wasn't doing that. I knew that a part of me needed someone as my foundation to help me get on my two feet. I truly believed Diego and I were doing that for each other.

"I don't know," he said.

I felt enraged by his answer. "That's not good enough." I then threw the picture at the wall behind him. It shattered on the ground.

Diego looked at the picture and then at me. I could see the anger in his eyes. He stormed at me. He grabbed me and slammed me against the wall. "What the fuck is wrong with you? How dare you disrespect the memory of Vanessa."

I could see all the hurt in Diego's eyes. "Because you love her over me. Why can't you just admit it. The thrill of me has worn off. Now you're realizing that Vanessa was a better choice of a lover," I said.

The anger in him melted away, and he dropped his hands. He stood there frozen like a statue. I could tell that he was shut down, and there was nothing that I could do. I just sighed heavily because what was I going to do.

Diego and I were showing the ugliness of each other, and we couldn't do anything to fix it. I walked around him and grabbed my wallet and keys. I walked to the door, and I turned around to see the sadness in his voice. This was his moment to say anything to keep me there, but he couldn't do it. I nodded, and I walked out of the apartment.

I got back to my place, and I crawled into bed. I felt all the pain wash over me, and I just wanted this pain to stop coming back over and over again. "I told you that you were nothing to him," Wes said, sitting on the edge of my bed.

"Go away!" I screamed.

He laughed and turned to me. "Tristian had moved on to someone better than you. He didn't even fight for you."

"Shut up!" I screamed into his face. "Leave me alone."

"Diego chose the wrong person. He should have stayed with Vanessa."

"You don't think I know that," I said. "You don't think I know I'll always be second best to Diego. I mean nothing to him," I said.

"I'm glad you finally figured it out," Wes said. "Sweet dreams." He stood up and walked out of my apartment.

I grabbed the pillow and curled up to it. It smelled just like Diego. I closed my eyes and began to cry. I wanted nothing more than for Diego to hold me and tell me it was going to be okay. Why was the one person that could fix it all be the same person causing this pain?

Chapter 4

Diego

"Why didn't you go after him?" Vanessa asked me, as I stood there frozen.

I just watched the love of my life walk out of those doors, and I honestly don't know if I'll ever see him again. I couldn't use my words, and it honestly kills me. I wanted nothing more than to tell him that he was wrong. I wanted to remind him that he was the only person to make me feel this way.

"Because maybe he's right. Maybe I should have been with you," I admitted.

She touched both sides of me face. "Diego, you know we wouldn't have worked out. We were holding on to a future that wasn't meant for us." She paused. "But you can have that with Diego."

"How do I fix this?" I asked.

"I think you know how," she said. "You're the man of action."

She was right. I was better with my hands. It was what I did best. I walked over and picked up the frame off the floor. I pulled the photo of Vanessa and I out of the frame and threw the frame in the trash.

The package contained a bunch of photos of Ash and I over the past six months. It was going to be one of my Valentine's Day gifts to him, but it seemed that I needed to give him this gift sooner. I pulled out a small frame that I bought, and I inserted the photo of Ash and I after our first month together.

It was a photo of us going hiking, and we took a selfie. I kissed him on the cheek, and his bright hazel eyes were beaming. It was honestly my favorite photos of us. I grabbed a trash bag and walked to my drawer. I pulled all of Vanessa's clothes out of the drawer and placed them in the bag. I stood up and snapped a picture of the empty drawer for Ash.

I grabbed the frame and my keys. I needed to fix things with Ash sooner than later. I drove over to his place because I wasn't going to let this fight leak into tomorrow. It was Valentine's Day tomorrow, and I wanted to spend the day filled with love.

I parked my car in front of his apartment. I looked at my glove box, and I thought about the small box that was in there. I thought maybe this was the time for me to give him the box, but I knew that it was meant for tomorrow. I had tomorrow planned, and I hoped not being an asshole wasn't going to ruin it.

I got out of the car, and I thought about what next step I wanted to take with Ash. I thought maybe that was why I had been all over with my emotions. It wasn't fare to Ash, but this was me making it right with him.

I opened Ash's door, and I looked into the darkness. "Ash?" I called out.

Ash lifted his head, and he looked at me with confusion. I saw his bloodshot eyes from the hall light. "Diego, what are you doing here?" he asked.

I turned the light on in his apartment. His eyes needed a second to adjust to the light. "I'm sorry," I said. "I know that I'm terrible with my words, and I know that's no excuse. I've tried over the past six months to make things good with us. I've spent the last six months proving to you that you're the most important person to me."

I walked over and sat on the bed. "And I've failed you."

He shook his head. "It's not all your fault. I saw Tristian today." My body started tensing up. He leaned over and touched my arm. "He didn't see me. He was with his new guy, and I thought about what his friend Wes had said. He told me that I was replaceable, and he was right. Tristian didn't fight for me back, not like I wanted him to. He just shrugged his shoulders and tossed me to the side," he said.

"Because the guy is an asshole."

He looked me in the eyes. "I know that, but there will always be a part of me that will still care what he thinks. That demon inside of me wants to remind me that I'm never going to be good enough. I looked around your apartment, and I don't see a single thing of me, and I believe it in our relationship."

"You're right. I should have done it sooner, but I hope that this will make it right," I said. I handed him the frame with the picture of us in it." I then pulled out my phone and showed him the picture of the empty drawer. "I cleaned out the last drawer of hers, and a part

26

of my gift to you tomorrow were pictures of us to put in each other's apartments."

He smiled and touched the frame. He leaned forward and kissed me on the lips. "Thank you," I said. "You didn't need to do this for me."

I shook my head. "I didn't do it for just you. I did it for us and our future. I never want to be with anyone else, Ash. I love you more than you could ever know." I leaned forward and captured my lips with his. It was filled with love, forgiveness, and promise for the future. Nothing in the world was better than this kiss from Ash.

Chapter 5

Diego

"You're going to burn the steak if you don't pay attention to it," Ash commented as he took a sip of his red wine.

I glared at him. "You can't really burn steak," I argued.

He smirked into his glass. "I don't want well done though," he said.

I rolled my eyes. "You're so difficult. Why don't you go set the table?" I asked.

"Fine," he said. I watched as he walked away from me and around the counter to set up the table. Ash had dressed up for me. He was wearing these tight blue dress pants with a white button up. It clung to his small frame and his ass spoke words to me.

"Why don't you stop staring at my ass and focus on the steaks," he suggested.

I coughed and turned back to the steaks. I blushed and looked down. "I wasn't staring at your ass," I replied.

"Shame. I've been staring at you all evening. I must say that I thought you in your workout gear was hot, but this is a whole different level," he commented. I was wearing gray dress slacks and a black button up.

I felt Ash pressing against me. "Do you understand how hard it has been for the last hour not to rip your clothes off and just have my way with you." I felt his hand slide up my ass, and I took in a heavy breath.

"I'm going to need you take your hand off my body right now."

"Or what?" he challenged me.

I turned to look at him. "Then you won't get this meal. Yes, you will get fucked later, but you wanted a romantic dinner for Valentine's Day, didn't you?" I asked.

He rolled his eyes. "Fine," he said. He stepped away and took a seat at the table. I chuckled because he looked adorable pouting.

I was extremely grateful he walked away because I felt my erection in my pants, and I was ready to fuck him right then and there on the kitchen counter. I took the steaks off the pan and on our plates.

I walked to the table, and I placed his plate in front of him. He poured us another glass of wine. We had a candle in between us, and I thought we had made it romantic. We didn't get each other chocolates or terrible cards. We didn't fill my apartment with red balloons. It was simple for the both of us.

He raised his glass. "Thank you for dealing with my baggage and loving me regardless."

He smiled too. "Thank you for showing me what love can truly be." We toasted and began to eat our meal. The small box had been on my mind all day, and

I just wanted to give it to him. I wanted his reaction more than anything.

We finished our meals, and I put the plates in the sink. I walked over and sat across from him. "Do you want to exchange gifts?" I suggested.

"Yes," he said. He walked into the bedroom and pulled out a box. He handed it to me. "You are the worst person to buy for," he said.

I rolled my eyes as I unwrapped the gift. I saw in the box that they were a new pair of boxing gloves. I smiled softly. "Thank you."

He shrugged. "I thought you might need new ones since you're going to be fighting more. I can't have my man out there boxing with shitty gloves," he commented. I knew he was trying to keep his emotions to a minimum, but I knew he was proud that he nailed it on the perfect gift.

I walked over to my gym bag and pulled out the small package that was in my glove box and another box. I handed him the bigger box first. "Here's your first gift," I said.

"First gift? I didn't know you were going to spoil me this much," he said. He unwrapped the gift, and it was a leatherbound journal. He looked at me a little astonished.

"I noticed that your writing journal was starting to get full, and I thought that you were in need of a new one," I commented.

He got up from his chair. I saw the tears in his eyes, and he leaned forward and captured my lips with his. It was a quick kiss. "Thank you so much." He took a seat and looked at the journal. "You've always been my biggest support, and I just am really grateful for that."

I lifted the boxing gloves. "You've done the same for me too," I agreed.

I felt the waves of nerves. I knew that this was going to be risky, but I needed to do it. I didn't want to think about it too much. "Here's your second gift," I said. I handed him the box.

He looked at it with skepticism before he began to open it. He took the wrapping off, and it was a black box. He opened it and lifted up a silver key. He looked at me confused. "Why are you giving me a key?" he asked. "I already have a key to your apartment."

I stood up and bent down in front of him. "This is a key to my new apartment. Our new apartment."

"Our?" he asked.

"Ash, we've both have been through so much together, and I don't want to be stuck in the past. You're right. This was my apartment with Vanessa, and I want a fresh chapter with you."

"Is this why you couldn't give up a drawer for me?" he asked.

I nodded. "Yeah. I guess I just wanted to have a few more days with the crazy fantasy of her before I finally closed the book on her."

He leaned forward and kissed me again. It was filled with passion and love. "I'm assuming that's a yes."

"Of course, it's a yes."

I stood up. "Good, I was worried that you were going to say no, and it was going to be an extremely awkward ending to this night."

He stood up, and he looked me in the eyes. "I had other plans for how this night was going to end," he said. I didn't know what he meant until his hand was on my crotch. The slight touch of Ash on me sent me wild.

I saw the arousal in his eyes, and I couldn't take it. I bent down and grabbed him by his ass and threw him over my shoulders in one swift movement. I carried him to the bedroom and threw him on the bed. "You're that horny, huh?" he asked.

I began to unbutton my shirt. "You have no clue how much you dressed up turns me on," I said. I got my shirt off, and I got on top of him.

I grabbed the shirt and pulled it open. I would buy him a new shirt tomorrow. I began attacking his neck with my teach. I felt the moans and whimpers coming out of Ash. He started grinding his crotch with mine. I felt both of us getting hard. I began to unbuckle his belt and unbutton his pants as I began making out with him.

I got off of Ash, and I stood at the edge of the bed. I grabbed the waist band of Ash's pants and briefs and pulled them down exposing Ash's hardened cock. I pulled his shoes and pants, causing Ash to be fully naked.

I unbuckled my belt and pushed my pants down. I began stroking my cock, and I felt the pre cum on my fingers. He raised an eyebrow. "Someone seems to be in the mood."

"I told you that I've been staring at your ass all night. I've wanted to stick my cock in there, and I couldn't wait any longer," I said.

I grabbed both of Ash's legs and pulled him closer to me. I pushed them up and laid them against my chest. I stroked myself a little bit before I positioned my cock at Ash's hole. "You ready?" I asked.

"I've been fingering myself all day for you," he said.

That was all I needed to hear before I inserted my cock inside his tight hole. We both let out a moan together. "God, I'll never stop loving this feeling," I said.

"I'll need you to start making some movements, please," he demanded. I heard the hunger in his voice.

"As you wish," I said. I began thrusting him as hard as I could. I loved the symphony of sounds that escaped Ash's mouth. The moans, groans, whimpers, and screams. I could hear them on repeat over and over again.

I reached forward and wrapped my hand around his cock. I began stroking him because I wanted both of us to get off.

A few minutes later, I felt myself getting close. "Ash, I'm close."

"Me, too. Hard! Hard! Hard!" he screamed in pleasure.

I gave him all I had as I continued to pound into him. The pleasure became too much, and I felt myself at the edge. I heard a scream come from Ash as I felt his hot cum coat all over my fingers. "Oh god!" That was all I needed before I began filling Ash up myself with cum.

I started slowing my rhythm as I finished inside of Ash. We both were breathing heaving for a moment. I slowly pulled out of Ash, and he made a little yelp noise. "Let me get you a rag," I said.

He grabbed my arm, and he pulled me down. "Give me a minute," he said.

He curled his body around me. "I just want to say that I love you, Diego. I've never loved someone as much as I love you. Thank you for making this Valentine's Day the best I've ever had. I'm sorry that yesterday was shit."

I shrugged. "We both let our past get the best of us. I love you, Ash. I never want to stop loving you. I'm excited for our future."

He leaned forward and kissed me, and I kissed him back. I wanted him to know that this felt like my first true Valentine's Day. I had such great moments with Vanessa, but they didn't compare to what I shared with Ash. I couldn't wait to see what was next for us. I knew there would be bumps and problems, but we would get through them. We were the love story that everyone dreamed of writer and even more, experiencing.

Secret Admirer

A Circle of the Red Scorpion

Short Story

by

Charlene Johnson

Chapter 1

"Hey, Mo, who's your date for Valentine's Day?" Nick Savage asked, as he studied the pool balls on the table, plotting his next move.

Moses Thorne smirked. "I haven't picked which lucky babe I'm going out with yet. I have so many in my little black book to choose from. It's going to be a hard decision since so many females are vying for my attention."

"If you have so many, how come we've never seen any of them?"

"Why would I subject them to the eye fucking they'd get from you?"

Nick laughed as he leaned on his pool cue and regarded him, a smug expression on his face. "You have nothing to worry about, Mo. The women you flirt with when we're out are definitely not my type."

Moses waved his hand in the air. "You're just jealous."

A slow smile spread across Nick's face. "Want to make a wager, demon?"

"On what?"

"That I'll have a beautiful, sexy Valentine's Day date before you."

"You're on, wolfman."

"Whoever has secured a date first wins."

"What's the prize?"

"Bragging rights."

"I'm good with that. I'd hate to take your money."

Nick leaned over the pool table and lowered the tip of his pool cue. "Right corner pocket."

"You won't make that shot," Moses scoffed.

"Watch me." Nick hit the cue ball and the solid red ball rolled smoothly into the right corner pocket. He followed it up by sinking the eight ball.

"Lucky shots," Moses grumbled.

Nick laid his pool cue on the table. "Admit it, I'm simply better at pool than you. I better start working on my date for Valentine's Day. The fourteenth is only two weeks away."

Moses grinned. "It's going to take you that long to find one, if you can."

Nick grinned. "My alpha pheromones are so strong they attract all the females, human and preternatural."

"They'll also attract the losers too. Be careful what you wish for."

Nick waved his words away. "I'm not worried. You, on the other hand should be."

"I'll have them lining up around the corner to go out with me."

"Good thing for you, we're staying at Broderick's penthouse. You might have a chance to pick someone up."

Moses smirked. "There are some real babes in Seattle. It won't be an issue."

"We'll see," Nick replied. "See you in the morning."

"Hey Nick, what about Sebastian? Are you asking him to participate in our little bet?"

"I'll let you ask him. Later."

Watching Nick leave the rec room, Moses' smile fell, and he slumped on the leather couch. He had no clue who he was going to ask out for Valentine's Day, but he'd never let Nick know it. As much as he bragged about being a ladies' man, he had a hard time finding a female, human or otherwise, he was terribly interested in. Contrary to what the other guys thought, he hated superficial females. He told the guys he liked them sleazy and easy, but it wasn't true.

Of course, Moses had his share of one night stands over the thousands of years of his existence. There had been one female he could have been serious about. Unfortunately, the timing wasn't right. Her name was Juliette. She was a beautiful, ebony haired slave who worked in a tavern on Broad Street in Savannah, Georgia. As soon as he saw her, he was instantly smitten. Had he not been tracking a murderous demon, he never would have met her.

Moses had come to Savannah in 1760, in pursuit of a shapeshifting demon, a stowaway he later found out was named Barnaby Cook. The demon arrived in Savannah harbor on the pirate frigate ship, The Devil's Lair. Moses waited for the demon to clandestinely disembark and followed him to the tavern. That's where he met Juliette.

Barnaby left behind a string of grisly murders in London blamed on an escaped tiger from a traveling circus in Westminster. Moses recognized the familiar scent when he examined the corpses in the city morgue. The killer was a demon. A demon who had the ability to shape shift. He was well associated with shapeshifting demons since he was one himself. His beast of choice was a fire-breathing green dragon. The difference between him and the other demon was he didn't prey on humans.

Moses suspected the demon was using the circus as a cover and decided to check it out. In those days, a traveling circus would erect temporary wooden structures with a performance ring in the middle. Exotic animals were kept outside of the structure in cages that spectators could view. He strolled past the cages that held lions, tigers, and hyenas. Was the demon one of those creatures?

He came back after hours and cloaked himself from view to test out his theory. Watching one of the circus crew check the animal cages before disappearing into one of the covered wagons, he waited. Minutes later, a human hand crept through the bars of a tiger's cage and slid open the iron bolt. The cage door swung open and a tall stocky man jumped down, immediately shifting into a tiger.

"Got you," Moses whispered and revealed himself.

The tiger's head swung in his direction and growled deep in his throat, his teeth bared and his stance menacing.

"I know what you are," Moses said. "I can't allow you to kill anyone else."

The tiger bounded away from him and headed into the city, before vanishing into one of the dark alleys. It would have been easy for Moses to shift into his dragon and fly above London to locate the tiger, but he couldn't take the chance of being seen.

Using his exceptional sense of smell to track him, he followed the tiger through the graveled streets of London to the harbor and down one of the docks.

There was a loud splash as one of the three masted frigates moved slowly away from the dock. Moses saw a man climbing up the slats of a wooden rope ladder and over the railing on the aft of the ship before disappearing. It was the demon he saw escape the animal cage.

As Moses watched the frigate gliding away, an older man with a ragged cap walked up the dock towards him.

"Can you tell me where that ship is going?" Moses asked.

The older man with snow white hair, regarded him critically before answering. "You mean, The Devil's Lair?"

"Yes."

"To the Americas. Why are you asking?"

"Someone I know is on that ship," Moses answered.

The older man put his hands on his hips, a frown deepening his brow. "Are you a pirate, too?"

"No. My friend and I have unfinished business."

"You won't be able to catch up with him, not until the ship docks on the other side of the ocean. Unfortunately, the next ship doesn't leave for two more days."

Moses nodded and handed him a handful of coins. "Thank you."

Moses smiled as he walked away from the docks. The demon could shift into any creature and hide. A fly, a cat, a rat. He didn't need to be on the ship to follow the demon. His dragon could do that just fine.

Chapter 2

Moses entered the tavern in Savannah, looking for the demon he tracked across the Atlantic Ocean. He scanned the tavern and found him sitting alone at a table in a dark corner, his back facing the door, drinking the mug of ale the barmaid sat in front of him.

At least, the demon wasn't out killing anyone. As soon as Moses saw him depart the tavern, he would end him before he killed again. He found a table on the opposite side, facing the demon and sat down.

"What can I get you, sir? A platter of food or a mug of ale?" a soft, feminine voice asked.

Moses turned his focus to the barmaid and froze. Wisps of coal black hair escaped from the white ruffled cap trimmed with a red silk ribbon. Her skin was mocha, and her eyes were golden brown. Her lips were full and inviting. His eyes roamed over the white cotton gown. It was simple but did not conceal the luscious curves that refused to be hidden.

He glanced at the table where the demon was drinking his ale and eating a platter of food. The demon wasn't going anywhere for now.

"I'll have a mug of ale." He grinned, his green eyes fastened on her.

She blushed and smiled back. "No food?"

"Not right now."

"Be right back."

Moses watched her walk away with appreciation and his body stirred. She was a beauty. He wished he had time to woo her, but his focus was on the shapeshifting demon he'd followed across the ocean. Perhaps, once he'd disposed of him, he could take some time off from demon hunting for a little romance.

The barmaid returned and placed the mug on his table. "Here you are. Anything else?"

"Your name."

"Juliette," she murmured, blushing again.

"A beautiful name," Moses replied.

"Thank you."

"I'm Moses."

She ignored his words. "Enjoy your ale."

Juliette turned to go, and he reached for her hand. "Don't go. Sit down and talk to me."

She looked from him to the tavern owner with a bald head and long gray beard who glared at her from behind the counter. She quickly pulled her hand away.

"I can't. I'm working."

"How long before you're through?"

"When the tavern closes at midnight." Juliette stole another glance at the tavern owner.

"Perhaps I can meet you afterward."

"I'm sorry. I can't."

"Why not?" Moses asked, his voice low. "Are you married?"

"No, I'm a…" She stopped when she saw the tavern owner heading towards them, wiping his hands on the dirty apron around his waist.

"Are you interested in her?" the man asked. "You can have her for a small fee."

Moses bristled and gazed at Juliette. She was staring down at the tavern floor. What was he missing?

"You can have her for the night." The tavern owner grinned, revealing rotten, uneven teeth. "I guarantee, she'll be worth your while."

Moses' heart seized as he stared at Juliette, who still would not meet his eyes. He leveled a murderous look at him.

"Is she your property?"

"Yes, she is."

Moses' jaws tightened. The bastard sold Juliette to his patrons. He wanted to kill the tavern owner where he stood, but the demon he was tracking suddenly stood up and was leaving the tavern.

He had to go, or he would lose him. He pushed his chair back and stood, looking at Juliette. "I'm sorry, I have some business that can't wait." He threw some coins on the table.

"The tavern is open until midnight if you change your mind," the tavern owner offered, putting his arm around Juliette's waist. "That is if she's still available. My Juliette is very popular with my patrons."

Moses watched the demon open the door and go outside. He looked at Juliette again. "I'm sorry," he whispered, and strode toward the tavern door.

When he was outside, he saw the demon walking briskly down the street three blocks away, then veer off the main street to enter a dark alley. Cloaking himself, he followed him through a series of alleys.

The sound of drunken singing caught Moses' attention. A drunken man stumbled into the alley, his footsteps unsteady. He also caught the attention of the demon, who stopped to look behind him. The demon stepped into a doorway, out of view. As the drunk man passed by, a large wolf emerged, stalking after him. The man didn't seem to notice the wolf and kept walking and singing, leaning heavily on the wooden building wall.

The wolf poised to strike. Moses had to act. He materialized in time to grab the wolf by the throat and throw him hard against the wall. It yelped in pain.

"Go!" Moses shouted to the drunk man, his eyes never leaving the wolf. "Get the hell out of here."

Startled, the man swung around and nearly fell. "What?"

"Go, goddammit, if you want to live."

The man stumbled back as he saw the wolf. "What the hell!"

"Go!" Moses commanded.

"Okay," the man answered, turning to stumble away.

Moses picked the disoriented wolf up by the throat and it clawed at his arm, but the animal's claws couldn't penetrate the dragon scales that suddenly covered it.

"Shift," Moses ordered, his green eyes glowing, his dragon near the surface. When the wolf didn't comply, he repeated the command. "Shift, or I'll crush your throat, demon."

The wolf instantly shifted into a man with black hair and beady dark eyes. Moses let go of him and he fell to the ground, gasping and coughing.

"You!" the demon exclaimed, his chest heaving.

"Yes, asshole. I've followed you from London to stop you from killing humans. What's your name?"

"I'm known as Barnaby...Cook," he gasped. "What...what are you going to do with me?"

"Ensuring you go back to Hell."

Chapter 3

Moses opened the door to the tavern after he returned from delivering Barnaby to the Archangel Michael, the leader of the warrior angels. Michael would decide whether to deliver the demon back to Lucifer for his judgement or send him to Sanctuary.

Sanctuary was the prison demons were sent to in Heaven when captured for committing a crime against humans. Inside the alabaster walls, a heavenly virtual reality scene and soft, angelic music repeated on a loop. Demons thrived on darkness, evil and the suffering of others. Their world was the antithesis of what Heaven stood for. The demons' dark energy drained after being subjected to centuries of heavenly bliss and ceased to exist.

Moses had befriended Michael after he left Hell and discovered they had one thing in common – stopping demons from harming humans. He'd worked with the archangel many times over the long eons they'd known each other.

Michael knew Moses had no interest in going to Hell for any reason. Since his father, Joash, and his mother, Terra, were elemental demons and part of Lucifer's inner circle, the chances of Moses seeing them would have been high. He and his father had a falling out thousands of years ago and he left Hell, vowing never

47

to return. He missed his mother but couldn't see her without also seeing his father.

But Moses didn't want to think about that now. He went back to the tavern to find Juliette.

He was disappointed when he didn't see her, and dread filled him as he surmised why. Irate, he strode to the bar counter where the tavern owner was talking with a patron.

The tavern owner grinned when he saw him. "You came back. You still want a go with Juliette?"

"Where is she?" Moses demanded, ignoring his question.

"She's upstairs. Second door on the right. She just finished with a patron."

"Bastard," Moses growled, in a low dangerous voice.

The tavern owner blanched. "Go on up. You can pay me when you're finished."

Moses took the steps two at a time, anxious to see Juliette, hoping she was alright. He knocked on her door, waiting for her to answer.

Juliette opened the door, an expression of shock on her face. "What are you doing here?"

"I came back to see you. To make sure you're alright."

"I'm fine," she said with resignation, wiping a dark curl back from her face.

"Can I come in?"

She stepped back for him to enter, then closed the door behind him.

Moses looked around the sparse room. There was a simple wooden table and spindle-backed armchair near the door. A wooden chest set beside a rumpled bed. He grimaced at the thought of what had taken place beneath the plain cotton sheets.

Juliette sat down on the bed, leaving the chair for him. He pulled the chair closer and took her hand. There were tears in her eyes.

"Why do you care what happens to me?" she asked, quietly. "You don't know me."

"I know we just met," he admitted, "but I sense you are special."

She shook her head. "I'm a slave, nothing more."

"That's not true," he insisted. "You're much more."

"Jedidiah owns me. I'm his property. I'll never be anything more."

"I can take you away from here."

A tear trailed down her cheek. "How, Moses?"

Moses stood up, pulling her up, too. "We can leave now."

She shook her head vehemently. "Jedidiah won't let me go."

"He won't know."

"What do you mean?"

"Is there anything you want to take with you?"

She frowned. "No. I don't want to take anything Jedidiah gave me."

"Very well." Moses wrapped his arms around her. "Close your eyes."

Juliette didn't question him, and he was glad. She would never understand what was about to happen. After he got her safely away, he would erase her memory and leave her to live her life as a free woman.

He was sorry he would have to leave her and regretted not making love to her even more. After what Jedidiah forced her to do, he wouldn't take advantage of her. It wasn't the right thing to do and he wasn't in the position to stay with her. The life he led was complicated. He hunted demons for a living and that was his life. There was no room for anything else.

In the end, Moses took Juliette north to an abolitionist and his family. She would be safe there. Before he took her to meet them, he erased her memory. When she was settled with his friends, he left her. It would have never worked out. She was human and would die of old age while he stayed the same. Better to leave her to live a good life.

That doesn't mean he forgot about her. He checked on her over her lifetime. She eventually got married and had children and grandchildren.

Moses left the rec room and went to find Sebastian. He was the one person he could always talk to, though there were things about his life he didn't even share with his best friend. Moses knew Sebastian would laugh when he told him about the bet with Nick and tell him what a supreme idiot he was. He needed him to do that.

Sure, it would be easy for Moses to find a date for Valentine's Day, but it wouldn't mean anything. He wasn't interested in another superficial fling. Not anymore. He needed something more, but would he find what he was looking for before Valentine's Day or would he have to settle for a female just to win the bet?

Chapter 4

Nick found Sebastian Pope in the command center, at one of the computers. He was eager to tell him about the bet he had with Moses. To make it work, he'd need Sebastian's help.

"Hey, Sebastian. It's late to still be working."

Sebastian looked up from the keyboard. "There have been some bizarre murders in New Orleans Mama Rose asked me to look into."

Mama Rose was Sebastian's adoptive mother. They've been together since his birth eight hundred years ago. She was an ancient witch and healer. When Mama Rose was concerned about murders with possible magical connections, he paid attention. Her instincts were never wrong.

"What type of murders?"

"Decapitations, organ removals, bloodletting. Someone appears to be trying to link the murders to the spirit of Marie Laveau."

Marie Laveau was the illegitimate offspring of a Creole mother and a free black man. Her mother and grandmother also practiced voodoo. Marie was a fortune-teller, healer, and voodoo priestess. She was a benevolent woman known for her hospitality and compassion. After her death, her daughter, Marie II, continued her work, drawing the same allegations.

Now, an unidentified person or persons twisted her legacy to commit murder.

"Marie Laveau is really dead, right?" Nick asked.

"Yes. So is her daughter. Although their spirits may still be present in the world, they would never commit murder. I knew them. Someone else is doing this."

"Are you going back home to investigate?"

"I'm just doing research on the murders. Once I get enough information, I'll talk to Broderick. He will probably send some of us down to check it out."

"Good, then you have time to help me," Nick said.

Sebastian raised an eyebrow. "Help you with what?"

"The joke I'm playing on Mo."

"Do I want to know?"

Nick chuckled. "It will be fun. I bet Mo I'd have a date for Valentine's Day before he did."

"Of course, he took you up on the challenge," Sebastian said ruefully.

"Damn skippy. I'm planning to pretend to be a secret admirer to fuck with him. I'll start texting him tonight. Once he gets the first text, it's going to drive him crazy. All you have to do is play it up big time. Encourage him to take it seriously. I'll do the rest."

"Are you really planning to find a date too?" Sebastian asked.

"Hell, no. I have no interest in dating anyone right now, although I'll have to pretend to so Mo won't get suspicious. Heads up. He's going to ask you to join the bet, too."

Sebastian rolled his eyes. "Great, just what I want to spend my time doing. I'm too busy collecting information on this case."

Nick chuckled. "Even you need some down time. Warlocks need to play too."

"I don't have great luck with women. It's exhausting, closing off my ability to hear their thoughts though most of the time I'm glad I can. Some of their thoughts are quite disturbing."

"I'm with you, brother," Nick replied.

"So, once you hooked Mo on his secret admirer, what happens next?"

"I'll string him along for a little while, but I promise I'll tell him before Valentine's Day."

****

Moses was sitting on a bar stool in a local bar not far from Broderick Devereaux's penthouse and chuckled as he recalled Sebastian's reaction when he asked him to join Nick's little bet.

"You're kidding, right?" Sebastian exclaimed. "I hate dating. You know that, Mo."

"Come on, Bas. Do it for me."

"No."

"I'll find you a date," Moses offered. "You won't have to do anything. We can double date if you want."

Sebastian smirked. "If we did that, my date would be hitting on you."

"That's not true," Moses insisted. "You sell yourself short."

"Really? The last time you and I went on a double date, my date spent more time talking to you than to me," Sebastian pointed out. "I could have left the restaurant and she wouldn't have noticed."

Moses laughed. "That's because you refused to talk to her. You got to communicate with your dates, Bas. That's how it works."

Sebastian shrugged. "Dating is not my thing."

He couldn't get a commitment out of Sebastian, but he was hopeful. If all else failed, he would harass him until he agreed.

Moses took a drink of his Dos Equis and scanned the bar. Not a single woman in the bar. All the women were paired up.

Oh well, he thought, *this place is a bust. There's always tomorrow. Perhaps, I'll try another bar.*

Moses was about to finish his beer and head back to the penthouse when his cell phone buzzed. A text message. It was probably Bas.

Restricted: *Hey, you, sexy, handsome demon.*

What the fuck? He instantly looked up from his cell phone and went on full alert. He looked around the bar. He didn't sense anyone suspicious but that didn't mean anything. Some preternaturals had the ability to cloak themselves just as he could. He began to type.

Moses: *Who's this?*
Restricted: *Your secret admirer.*
Moses: *I don't have one.*
Restricted: *You do now.*
Moses: *Have I ever seen you?*
Restricted: *Yes.*
Moses: *Where did we meet?*
Restricted: *Many places. You are unforgettable.*
Moses: *I wish I could say the same about you, but I'd have to meet you first.*
Restricted: *In due time. I'll text again soon, handsome.*

Moses didn't reply. He got no more texts. He was intrigued yet very wary. Whoever sent the texts knew what he was. Broderick and their team had many enemies who would like to bring them down and silence them permanently. Protecting the world from other preternaturals came with deadly risks the Circle of the Red Scorpion team vowed to accept.

The timing of the texts was odd. Was it a true secret admirer or an enemy? Either way, he needed to find out.

Moses finished his beer and tipped the bartender before leaving the bar, heading back to the penthouse. Nick might be able to track the texts.

****

Claudette Bradley sat at a table nearby with her date, watching Moses, who was laser focused on his cell phone. Who was he texting? A girlfriend? He was very intent as he frowned at the screen. Good lord, he was handsome. She hadn't expected that. His milk chocolate brown skin, curly black hair and sparkling emerald eyes. She'd come to Seattle to find him. He was her current assignment.

At first, she balked at having to tail him but after seeing him in person, her interest in him increased and not just because she had to. Her orders were to survey and report back. There were a few things she knew about him. First, he was a demon and an incredibly special one. He was one of a kind. An elemental demon with the abilities of fire and earth. Second, he was a member of Broderick Devereaux's Circle of the Red Scorpion, a team of paranormal warriors. And third, he could be extremely dangerous, though studying him now, he didn't appear to be. But looks were deceiving and she was aware of that.

"Ready to go, Claudette?" her date asked. "I have an early meeting in the morning."

She smiled at her date. "Of course, it's pretty dead in here anyway."

Claudette left the bar and walked down the street to her date's Mercedes. She'd seen what she needed to. Although she was told not to approach him, it was one order she didn't plan to obey.

Chapter 5

On his way to Nick's bedroom, Moses' cell phone buzzed again. He pulled it out of his pocket and looked at the screen.

Restricted: *I see you made it home, handsome.*

What the hell! Moses thought. Is someone watching him? His wariness increasing, he began to type.

Moses: *Why are you following me?*
Restricted: *I can't help myself. I'm so attracted to you.*
Moses: *Who the hell is this?*
Restricted: *I told you I'm a secret admirer.*
Moses: *If you're not willing to meet, stop texting me.*
Restricted: *I don't want to stop.*
Moses: *Then we must meet.*

He waited for a response, but one didn't come right away. Just as he was shoving his cell phone in his pocket, it buzzed.

Restricted: *Okay. I'll meet you tomorrow night at the bar I saw you at tonight.*
Moses: *I'll be there.*

Moses knocked on Nick's bedroom door, unwilling to wait until the morning to talk to him. He needed to know who was texting him. Nothing sparked his interest like the texts had in some time. Could it be a female and not an enemy? He hoped it was the former not the latter.

Nick opened the door, wearing nothing but gym shorts, glaring at him, the room behind him dark. "What the fuck to you want, demon? I'm trying to sleep."

Moses barged in, ignoring his friend. Nick was always grumpy when he got woken up. The alpha needed his beauty sleep.

"I got text messages I need you to look at." He tapped the text message app and handed his cell phone to Nick. "I need to know who the fuck sent them. Can you track them?"

Nick read the text string and ground his teeth to stop from grinning. "It looks like you have an admirer. What's the big deal?"

Moses frowned. "Whoever it is knows I'm a demon, asshole. Doesn't that alarm you? It could be an enemy."

Nick yawned. "You're safe now. Can't it wait until the morning?"

"No, wolfman, it can't."

Nick blew out a breath. "Shit, Mo. Why the urgency? This place is warded. No one can get to us, thanks to Sebastian."

59

"But if it's an enemy, we need to know," Moses insisted. "And how did they get my private cell phone number?"

"What if it's a potential date for Valentine's Day?" Nick teased.

Moses frowned. "That's not funny."

"Kind of is. Come on, Mo. You don't really think it's an enemy."

"I don't know."

"You have to admit the timing is great. You need a date to win our bet and it looks like you might have one. If she's preternatural like us, she could rock your world."

"I'm not ruling it out, but I have to know if it's real." Maybe he was making too much of it.

"There's always your little black book."

"True."

Nick laughed. "I just had another thought. Your secret admirer could be a guy."

Moses grinned. "Well, that wouldn't be surprising. I am devastatingly handsome."

"God," Nick exclaimed, rolling his pale green eyes. "What a fucking ego! Tell me again why I put up with you?"

"Because you love me."

Nick scowled, pulling on a t-shirt. "Let's go, asshole."

Sebastian was still sitting in front of one of the large monitors when they entered the command center.

"What are you still doing in here, man?" Nick asked.

Sebastian pivoted to them. "I'm getting ready to sign off. What are you two doing?"

Nick pointed to Moses. "Our friend here got a text message from a secret admirer and he wants me to find out who it is."

"It could be an enemy," Moses pointed out quickly.

"An enemy that calls you handsome and sexy?" Nick asked.

"You forgot to add demon," Moses countered.

Nick shrugged. "A term of endearment."

Sebastian raised an eyebrow. "Interesting."

Moses glared at Nick. "Let's get on with it."

Nick put his hands up. "Okay, okay." He sat down beside Sebastian and logged on to the other computer. "There's no guarantee I'll be able to pinpoint the sender. Your secret admirer could be using a burner phone."

"Try, dammit," Moses growled.

Nick glanced at him. "Easy, demon. I told you I'd try."

"Why are you so perturbed, Mo?" Sebastian asked, trying to pretend concern but also feeling traitorous, knowing who sent the texts.

"I don't like being fucked with if that's what's happening."

"I told Mo, it was probably quite innocent," Nick said, as he opened a tracking program and began to type.

61

"Whoever it was knew I made it back to the penthouse," Moses insisted.

"It could be some young lady likes you, Mo," Sebastian placated. "Let's not jump to conclusions."

Moses looked over Nick's shoulder as he worked. "Find anything?"

Nick glanced at him. "Nothing. Like I told you before, these traces often lead to dead ends. The texts are coming from an untraceable number. I can't track it back from your number. I'm sorry."

"Thanks for trying, wolfman. I guess I'll blow off the meeting with my secret admirer tomorrow night." Moses replied, his disappointment clear, and took his cell phone from the table. "See you guys in the morning. I'll report the texts to Broderick when I get up."

"I'll do it for you," Sebastian offered. "I have an early phone meeting with him."

Moses nodded. "Thanks."

"We need to tell him, Nick," Sebastian said, after Moses left the command center. "He's taking it way too seriously. We don't need to get Broderick spun up thinking someone is threatening us."

"You're right," Nick replied, "but as much as Mo has fucked with us over the years, it was time we get a little payback."

"Don't get me wrong, I like pulling a practical joke on him as much as you do but your text messages seem to have caught him off guard. I think it's more than thinking the sender is a threat."

Nick was surprised. "You really think so?"

"I do. I've noticed his interest in casual dates has waned of late. I think he's been watching the other guys pair up and perhaps he wants that too. First, it was Drake and Ebony. Then, Broderick and Elise reuniting and Dominic getting married to Chantelle. There's also Chase's on again, off again relationship with Fallon. He's going to be hurt and a little pissed if he finds out you're his secret admirer."

Nick contemplated Sebastian's words. He loved Mo like a brother. Hell, Mo was more of a brother to him than his own. He hadn't talked to his older brother, Cedric, in years. None of the team even knew about him, not even Broderick. Cedric left the pack twenty years before their father was killed. No one in the pack ever mentioned him. As far as he and the pack were concerned, Cedric was dead to them. He didn't even know if his brother was still alive.

Nick never thought Mo would settle down. He hadn't ever mentioned it. There was much the team didn't know about his past. Not even Sebastian. Mo never talked about his life in the demon world or his parents. It was clear there were many hidden layers to his friend.

"Maybe you're right," Nick admitted.

"How do you want to tell him?"

"Why tell him? I just won't text him again. Once he doesn't receive another text, he'll let it go."

"What about the meeting tomorrow night?"

"He said he wasn't going. We're in the clear."

"Okay," Sebastian agreed. "We'll play it your way."

Chapter 6

"Did you set eyes on Moses?" A male voice in the darkness asked, startling Claudette.

"Yes, papa," she answered, sitting up in her bed. "I saw him earlier tonight."

"Good," the voice rasped.

"Is there anything else you want me to do?"

"Not yet. Just watch him for now."

"I will," she replied.

Claudette hated when her father showed up that way. It always scared the shit out of her. He told her it was risky for him physically to come to her and used astral projection to communicate. She wanted to ask him what his interest was in Moses but knew better. Her father didn't like to be questioned.

She planned to go to the bar again tomorrow evening alone, hoping Moses would be there. She needed to know more about him, not having much luck on her own. The group he worked with kept low profiles. Each of them had a public persona that was readily available online but nothing regarding their preternatural existences. It was something they kept well hidden.

Claudette had no idea how long she would be in Seattle. Her father used her to be his eyes and ears all over the world. He may call her away soon and she didn't want to leave without seeing Moses.

She laid back down, pulling the comforter up and closed her eyes, her thoughts focused on the gorgeous, sexy demon that she couldn't forget.

****

Moses woke up the next morning as unsatisfied and frustrated as he was when he went to sleep. The texts he received still bothered him and left him unsettled. They seemed innocent but someone was tracking his movements. Shouldn't he be concerned? Regardless, he decided not to go to the appointed meeting.

He needed a distraction, so he planned to sit down with Sebastian and go over the information he was collecting on the murders in New Orleans. Hopefully, once Sebastian talked to Broderick, he would more than likely send them down to investigate.

Sebastian and Nick were eating breakfast in the kitchen when he came out of his bedroom.

"How's it going, Mo?" Nick asked.

"I'm okay," he answered.

"Good to hear," Sebastian added.

"I wanted to see what data you found on the murders."

Sebastian nodded. "I can show you after breakfast."

Moses got a bowl and spoon, the jug of milk and his favorite cereal and settled in the chair across from Nick and Sebastian. He ate his cereal quietly, the normal banter he shared with the guys subdued.

After breakfast, Nick left the penthouse and drove his Harley out of Seattle to check in with one of the local wolf packs residing north of the city. He wouldn't be back until the evening.

Moses spent the day with Sebastian, reading through police reports and newspaper articles. It was dark when Moses pushed away from the computer monitor.

"There's definitely something strange about the murders. Marie Laveau's spirit had nothing to do with this."

"That's what I told Nick," Sebastian agreed.

"We have to get down there and figure out who's really doing this."

"I'm going to call Mama Rose now and see if she has any more information. What are your plans?"

"I'm going down the street to one of the bars and drink a few beers. I won't be out too late, unless I get lucky," Moses beamed.

"You're back to normal," Sebastian teased.

"Nearly. I decided not to worry about those texts," he said. "I'm going to go out and have some fun. Are you sure you don't want to come?"

"Positive. See you later."

****

Moses walked down the busy street toward the bar he went to last night, the text messages still on his mind. He told the guys he wasn't going to meet his secret admirer, but he lied. He had to find out who it was.

He opened the bar door, scanning the bar carefully then froze. A stunning black woman was sitting alone at a table near the back wall, staring back at him with open curiosity. He'd once thought he'd never meet another woman as beautiful as Juliette again, but he was wrong. It took centuries but he finally did.

The delectable woman had long multicolored braids and honey brown eyes. Her full, perfect lips were painted a deep red. His eyes roamed over her body wrapped in a black leather halter dress and finished off with matching stilettos. Her legs were crossed gracefully, a long length of her sexy thighs exposed to his view. She was a total knockout. He was caught off guard and so was his cock, which was starting to strain against his black jeans.

Was she his secret admirer? God, he hoped so. He didn't sense she was preternatural and that gave him pause. If she was his secret admirer, how did she know about him?

Moses was debating whether to approach her when she motioned to him. Decision made. He was going in. He smiled and headed to her table.

"Hello," he greeted.

Claudette smiled and put out her hand. "I'm Claudette Bradley."

He shook her hand. "Moses Thorne, although you already know my name."

She looked surprised. "Excuse me?"

Moses chuckled. "You don't have to pretend. I know you're the one who sent me those text messages. That's why we're both here."

Claudette was confused. "I'm not sure what you're talking about."

He lifted a confused eyebrow. "You didn't send the text messages?"

She grinned, her dimples deepening. "No, but I'll send you one now if you want me too." She pulled her cell phone out of her clutch. "What's your number?"

Moses laughed. "That's not necessary."

Claudette set down her cell phone. "Sounds like you were planning to meet someone. I was going to ask you to join me. It's so pathetic for a woman to sit alone in a bar."

"I'm not meeting anyone," he answered, and sat down across from her.

"Good." She waved the barmaid over.

"What can I get you?" The barmaid asked Moses.

"Dos Equis," Claudette answered instead. "And I'll have another martini."

"Coming right up."

Moses was surprised. "How did you know that?"

"I was in the bar last night with a date and saw you. I hoped you'd come back in tonight. I left my date at home."

"Do you have a boyfriend?" he asked.

"No. He's just a business acquaintance."

"What line of work are you in?" Moses asked.

"I'm an art dealer. I travel the world buying unique artwork for my clients."

"Sounds interesting."

She sipped her martini. "What about you? What do you do?"

"I create video games and game apps."

"That sounds like fun."

"It can be," he replied. "Do you live here in Seattle? I've never seen you around here before."

"I have a condo in LA, but I'm rarely there. I've been living out of a suitcase."

"I can empathize with that. I have a flat in New York City, but I'm never there either. My business keeps me away a lot."

Claudette reached across the table and placed her hand on his. "It seems we have some things in common."

Moses flashed a slow, seductive smile. "I believe we do."

Chapter 7

Moses was whistling as he entered the penthouse a little after midnight. Nick and Sebastian were watching Cops on the seventy-inch 4k television.

"Those cops are so lame," Nick pronounced. "Not one of them could take down one of our perps. They can barely handle a drunk driver."

"I can't argue with that," Sebastian agreed.

"Hey guys," Moses greeted.

Nick and Sebastian turned to look at him.

"Back so early?" Nick asked.

"The bar was pretty dead tonight."

Nick tapped his watch. "Time's a-wasting."

Moses grinned. "I still have time. What about you?"

Nick sat back on the couch. "I'm weighing my prospects. I'll make a decision soon."

"Good for you, wolfman. I'm going to bed. See you both tomorrow."

Nick and Sebastian looked at each other and at Moses as he walked down the hallway.

"He's mellow," Sebastian observed.

"He sure is," Nick agreed. "I wonder why."

"No clue, but I'm glad to see it. Thank god, that text message fiasco is dead. No more practical jokes for a while, Nick."

"Deal, although life will be boring if I can't give Mo shit."

Moses was smiling when he entered his bedroom and started to undress. He had a great night, and he was going to have another one this evening. He had a date with Claudette. They were going to that new restaurant not far from the bar. After that, who knew?

He was amazed that he finally found a female he had some things in common with. She was so perfect. She was intelligent, funny and oh so sexy. They spent hours talking about pretty much everything – accept what he was. That was a conversation they might not ever have but he was happy to just be a regular guy for once.

Moses had no intention of telling Nick or Sebastian about Claudette. She was his little secret, at least for now and the thought excited him.

His cell phone buzzed, and he picked it up immediately.

Claudette: *I had a great time.*
Moses: *I did too.*
Claudette: *Can't wait to see you tonight.*
Moses: *Me either.*
Claudette: *Goodnight, Moses.*
Moses: *Goodnight, Claudette. Sweet dreams.*

He laid down on his bed and closed his eyes, feeling fortunate at the unexpected turn of events. When he fell asleep, he dreamed of Claudette.

The next evening was just as great as the night they met, and they saw each other every night for nearly two weeks. Valentine's Day was tomorrow, and Moses booked a hotel room by the harbor and ordered dinner to be delivered to the suite.

For days, Nick had been asking him who his date was, and he refused to answer. He didn't even tell him where they were going on their date. As far as he was concerned, what he shared with Claudette was no longer part of the bet, it was real.

****

Claudette stared at herself in the mirror, hoping Moses liked the red velvet off the shoulder cocktail dress she bought to wear for their Valentine's Day date. She was nervous and she knew why. This night was going to be different. Moses booked a hotel room, and it meant their relationship was moving to the next level. So far, they had only kissed but those kisses weren't chaste by any stretch of the imagination. They were hot and held the promise of so much more. Last night she almost begged him to stay with her, but she was afraid her father would make an unannounced appearance and she couldn't risk it. If he found out her interest in

Moses was more than a job, his punishment would be severe.

"You look beautiful, daughter. Going out tonight?"

Claudette jumped and turned to see the black translucent shape of her father in the shadows.

"It's Valentine's Day, father. I have a date. Why are you here?"

"To tell you this will be your last night in Seattle. I need you in New Orleans by tomorrow evening."

Claudette's heart lurched. "A new assignment?"

"Yes. Your mother contacted me. She needs you there."

She hadn't talked to her mother in months. They had a disagreement about her continuing to work for her father. Her parents had been estranged for a long time and her mother said her father was taking advantage of her and she needed to make a clean break. She loved them both but was beginning to understand what her mother was saying. She realized she'd have no life if she continued helping him.

"Very well, father," Claudette replied, trying to hide her disappointment. "I'll leave in the morning."

She went into the bathroom and started applying makeup as her tears threatened to ruin it. She wiped her tears away. Her time in Seattle was always supposed to be temporary, but she wasn't ready to go. The thought of leaving Moses pained her in a way she didn't know was possible, but she had no choice. She would have to make the most of her last evening with Moses because after tonight she would not see him again.

Chapter 8

"Do you want to have drinks in the bar before going up to the room? We don't really have to. There's a fully stocked bar in the hotel suite," Moses told Claudette, as he handed his car keys to the hotel valet and put his arm around her.

"No, I can wait until we get to the suite."

Claudette looked around the upscale hotel, admiring its old-world elegance with its large glittering chandeliers and two grand staircases that led to its world-class restaurant. Moses was checking in at the lobby counter while she tried to shake off a sudden wave of nerves. It was her last night with Moses. Tomorrow, she would be gone.

She felt his hand in hers and looked up, smiling at him, as he led her to the VIP elevator. He slid the key card into the slot, the elevator door opened, and they stepped inside.

Moses immediately pulled her into his arms. "I couldn't wait until we got upstairs."

Claudette wrapped her arms around his neck. "I'm glad." She lifted on her tiptoes and kissed him.

Moses pulled her tighter, as her curves pressed into him, deepening their kiss, then lifted his head to stare down at her, his eyes pools of emerald fire.

"Did I tell you how beautiful you are tonight?"

Claudette scarlet lips turned up in a naughty smile. "I don't believe you did. Did I tell you that you are red carpet ready in that black Armani suit?"

He kissed her bare left shoulder and then the right. "No, baby, but I like hearing it."

The elevator door opened to an impressive suite with midcentury-inspired furnishings, contemporary art, and a series of floor to ceiling windows that looked out over the Puget Sound. The lights in the suite were low, the main illumination coming from the candles placed throughout the room. A large mylar heart balloon floated above the red rose centerpiece on the small oval dining table.

"Lovely," Claudette murmured, walking into the suite.

"Would you like some champagne?" Moses asked, striding to the dining table in front of the windows and pulled the bottle from the ice bucket.

"Not really," she replied, as she walked sensuously toward him.

He placed the bottle back in the bucket and turned to her in surprise. "Would you like something stronger?"

Shaking her head, she placed her hands on his chest and slowly backed him up against the window. "The only thing I want is you."

Claudette unbuttoned his suit jacket and started on his dress shirt. She kissed the smooth skin of his toned chest as she continued until his shirt was open. She was aware it was a bold move on her part, but she didn't have time to waste. She hoped Moses wasn't turned off by her aggressiveness. That concern was quickly allayed when her hand glided over the front of his trousers and squeezed. He was already hard.

He moaned and thrust against her hand. "Oh, fuck!"

"I hope you don't think I'm too bold," she whispered against his chest, her tongue tracing a circle around his right nipple.

Moses closed his eyes and leaned his head back on the window, his arms pressed against his sides. "No," he sucked in a breath. "I fucking love a woman who knows what she wants and goes for it."

Her hands got busy unbuckling his belt and unzipping his trousers, pushing them and his boxer briefs down his thighs.

Opening his eyes, Moses kicked off his shoes and his trousers and briefs followed. Unfastening his cufflinks, he shrugged out of his jacket and shirt. The only things he had on were his socks.

Claudette stood back and admired his deliciously brown skin and taut, honed body. He was exceptional. Her eyes strayed to his erection and licked her lips, eager to wrap them around him.

Moses pushed off the window, but she pushed him back. "Don't move," she purred, and walked over to one of the dining chairs.

The cool surface of the window against his body did nothing to quell the fire that was building inside him.

He hadn't been intimate with a female in months and being inside Claudette nearly caused him to ignore her.

She pulled her dress over her head, exposing her full breasts and cleanly shaved sex, leaving on her black stiletto heels. She threw her dress over the back of the chair and walked seductively towards him. Her breasts bounced and her hips swayed with each step.

Moses was mesmerized by the stunning Nubian seductress who moved closer and closer, forcing himself to remain still. Her long braids rubbed against her dark nipples and he watched them tighten. His cock reacted.

When Claudette reached him, she slid her hands down his chest as she lowered to her knees, her hands continuing to caress his skin as she went. Smiling up at him, her hands moved back up his thighs before gripping his slim hips, and leaning in to take him into her mouth, her long braids caressing his thighs, adding to the erotic sensation. Moses' body flexed off the window, but she pushed him back, as she devoured him inch by inch.

Moses pressed his hands against the window so hard, he thought it would break under the pressure. Claudette's remarkable mouth took the length of him down to the base. She slowly slid up to suck on the swollen head and back down. Watching her bob up and down on his swollen cock brought sensations racing up his thighs to gather into a swirling firestorm in his balls, robbing him of breath. He'd never felt so much pleasure.

"Claudette, baby, that's enough," he groaned.

She lifted her head enough to speak. "Not until you come," she said, and took him back in her mouth.

"Shit!" he moaned, as he felt his release building.

Claudette felt him spasm and held on to him as he came, swallowing the warm spicy evidence of his climax. When she lifted her head, she was amazed that he was still hard.

"Sweet Jesus," he breathed, "that was unbelievable, but we're not done yet," he groaned, pulling her up and turning until she was against the window. He gripped her ass and lifted her up high enough to lower her onto his cock.

Claudette cried out as he filled her, pumping into her, her ass bumping the window each time he moved. She wrapped her legs around his waist, riding the waves of his deep thrusts.

The bite of Claudette's stiletto heels pressing into his ass ignited his fervor, sparring him on. Her tight pussy pulsated around him, causing his cock to swell even more. He shifted her legs over his shoulders, her ass in his hands and her back against the window.

"Stroke your clit, baby. I want your gorgeous eyes on me when you come."

She did as he asked, the pressure of her fingers and the length of his thick cock filling her to bursting took her over the edge. Her eyes widened and never left his as the orgasm swept over her. Through her erotic haze, she felt him stiffen and felt the warmth of his release inside her.

Moses slowly let her legs slide to the floor, but he held onto her, not ready to let her go.

When they finally stirred, he took her hand and led her from the living room to the bedroom, past the unopened champagne bottle and empty place settings.

He laid down on the bed, pulling her with him. "You are a remarkable woman."

She kissed the side of his neck. "You are an amazing man."

"I have to confess, I've avoided going out on Valentine's Day," Moses said. "I thought it was an over-commercialized, hyped up holiday. But you made it so memorable, I don't think I'll ever look at it that way again."

Claudette buried her face against his chest as tears threatened, knowing it would be the only Valentine's Day she and Moses would share.

"I will never forget it either."

There was a knock at the hotel door.

"It must be our dinner," he said. "Are you hungry?"

She lifted her head and gave him an impish grin. "Not for food."

He laughed and let her go to get off the bed. "Be right back."

Claudette turned over on her stomach, her emotions raw and her heart aching. She didn't want to leave him, now that she knew he was the one for her. But she refused to dwell on leaving him. She and Moses had the rest of the night and she planned to savor every minute.

Chapter 9

Moses woke up, a satisfied smile on his face. What a glorious night! He stretched enthusiastically and turned to gaze at the beautiful woman he spent the magnificent night with. She wasn't there. He frowned. He'd booked the suite through the weekend and planned to ask her to stay with him but that wouldn't be happening.

He could still feel her against his skin. He wished he could tell her how much their time together meant to him. It wasn't only because of the sizzling hot sex. In the nearly two weeks they'd spend together, he'd come to care deeply for her. That's why her leaving so abruptly hurt. Having lived for thousands of years, he'd met every kind of female and none ever came close to being as compatible and utterly perfect as Claudette. In his heart, he knew she was the one he'd been waiting for.

Getting out of bed, he searched the hotel room for a note and found one by the table near the elevator door.

Moses,

I'm sorry I had to leave you so early. I got a text this morning from a major client. I'm leaving for Paris in a few hours. I wish we had more time. Last night was the most amazing of my life and I'll never forget you. I hope we meet again.

Take care,

Claudette

"Well shit," Moses exclaimed, with disappointment and frustration. How had he not heard her leave? He went to the foyer table, retrieving his cell phone to call her. It went straight to voicemail. She was probably already in the air. He'd go to the penthouse and try to call her again later.

He checked out of the hotel since there was no reason to stay. He drove over to the penthouse and parked the car Broderick left for the team in the underground parking lot.

When he entered the penthouse, voices were coming from the command center, so he headed in that direction. Broderick Devereaux was sitting at the conference table with Nick, Sebastian, and Dominic Rinaldi. He was surprised to see Dominic, who had been living in Italy since he and Chantelle were married.

"Hey guys," he greeted, as he sat down beside Nick. "Dominic, it's nice to see you."

"Likewise," Dominic answered.

"How's marriage treating you?"

Dominic smiled. "Couldn't be better."

Nick pivoted in his chair. "Did you have a nice Valentine's Day? You're looking very relaxed."

"I did. How was yours?"

Nick looked at Sebastian and back to him. "My date cancelled at the last minute. I guess that means you won the bet."

"In more ways than one," Moses grinned.

"Who is the mystery woman?" Nick asked. "You never told us."

"No one you know."

"Are we going to meet her?"

"She flew to Paris this morning on business. I'm not sure when she'll be back."

Moses wasn't ready to talk about Claudette. He was still confused and hurt by why she didn't wake him before she left to say goodbye. He needed answers.

"What's going on?" he asked, changing the subject. "It must be important."

"Sorry, we didn't wait for you," Broderick said. "The guys told me you were out. Sebastian was briefing us on the information he collected on the recent murders in New Orleans. It's clear we need to do some groundwork there. We were also discussing our plan to investigate Dominique Malveaux's death. Now that Chantelle is safe, we need to find out who killed her. I'm assigning the two cases to you and Sebastian. I want you to go to New Orleans in the morning and get started."

Sebastian grinned. "I told Mama Rose we're coming to visit."

Moses pumped his fist in the air. "Fucking awesome. I can't wait to leave."

The usual excitement Moses always felt when he was on a case shifted his mind from Claudette. He had no idea when he would hear from her again. A new assignment was just what he needed to keep negative thoughts and doubts from invading his mind.

Moses stopped packing later that evening to call Claudette. Straight to voicemail again. He left her a message.

"Hi Claudette. I hope you had a nice flight. I wanted to let you know, I'll be traveling for at least a few weeks, but I'll have my cell phone. Please call me when you get a chance. I want to thank you again for a spectacular Valentine's Day. I look forward to hearing from you soon. I miss you."

Moses finished packing and the next morning he and Sebastian flashed to New Orleans. The sounds and smells of the city he adopted as his own always made him feel good. He and Sebastian would be busy for the next several days trying to get leads to the recent murders and find out who killed Dominique.

As Moses and Sebastian entered Mama Rose's shop, Claudette's lovely face and the Valentine's Day passion they shared filled his mind. If he didn't hear from her before he and Sebastian were done with these cases, he would flash to Paris and find her. He grinned, optimistic he would hear from Claudette again very soon.

My Very Own Valentine

My Very Own SuperHero

Short Story

by

D. S. Tossell

Chapter 1

My heart is hammering in my chest, as I clinch my textbooks closer towards me. My bottom lip trembles, but I catch it with my teeth, the one habit my mother hates that I do. The bell rings right above my head, making my body jump and my skin come alive with goosebumps.

The halls of Shallow Valley high school become what I'm used to, busy and full of people that I've known most of my life. I wave a few hellos, but keep my eyes on the classroom just across from me.

I had escaped from class a few moments early, hoping to get to my locker in time to apply a little makeup. Now I feel stupid, as I stand here with the same textbooks, starring at a closed door that holds everything important to me.

Today is the day.

The door opens and just as more students are milling out of the classroom, my view is instantly blocked when my best friend of over ten years appears in front of me.

"Are you waiting for him?"

I try and peer around her, but her large wad of hair remains further in my way when she stands on her tiptoes. I'm tall, always have been, and thanks to my father, always will be. Leaving Nancy normally at my shoulder most days.

"Is he going to be coming from that classroom?"

"He told me that this is his last period. But I was sort of hoping to find him *alone*." I give her my best side eye, but she simply disregards it, turning around to see if she can spot him herself.

"Oh, is that him?"

I peer over her head, and my heart stops when I spot Alston coming out of the science lab. His hair is dark-- daker than normal, his brown eyes more vibrant. At six foot tall, he's the best wide receiver the school has. Which is seriously saying something. He spots me and give me his famous chin nod, something that has me clutching the textbooks even closer to my chest.

Questions I've never asked myself flow around my head.

Did I wear deodorant today?
Did I brush my teeth?
What is my name again?

"Gwen. I think he's coming this way." My heart hammers rapidly as he approaches, a large megawatt smile appears on his face, making my cheeks redden.

"Hey." He stops just a foot away, and oh God, I can smell his cologne from here. "Thanks for meeting me." He peers down at Nancy and give her his famous smile, the one the cheerleaders have given a cheer for.

I may or may not have memorized it.

"N-no problem. I got your note that you wanted me to meet you here, so here I am. I had biology last period, so I had to leave a tad bit early to get here in time, but it was no biggie."

God Gwen, shut up!

"Oh uh, thanks. So, I asked Matilda to ask you to come here because I need a huge favor."

"Name it, anything. I could do anything, be down for anything." More red. Ugh, definitely getting more red. Nancy steps in front of me, her thick lashes come into my peripheral view as she tries to get me to stop yammering, but it's not exactly helping.

"Right. So, you're friends with Joanna Wilder, right?"

Pitfall. Face plant.

"What?"

"Joanna? She's on the swim team with you right?"

"Oh, yeah she is."

His smile grows wider and he actually looks…. wait is he blushing right now?

"The reason I'm asking, is because I was hoping to ask her to the Valentine's Day Dance. I don't have any classes with her, but we've been neighbors for a while. I thought it would be pretty weird to ask her out at home. Would you tell her to meet me somewhere?"

My stomach drops into the bottom of my feet. The sweat that was once forming across my back is now frozen to my skin.

Alston is not here for me. He's not trying to ask me to the dance tomorrow night. He's here to ask me to be his pimp.

Alston's brown eyes deepen as he looks me up and down. Nancy, being the amazing person she is, steps forward and handles the rest of the conversation meant for me. I don't hear much, too much ringing in my ears for me to hear the whole conversation, but I don't miss the fact that Nancy promises that I will definitely give Joanna the message.

Once Alston leaves, Nancy turns and gives me a look of pity. I turn and throw my textbooks into my locker, closing it shut with a loud slam. I begin walking out of the school, only to be pulled back by Nancy's arms.

"Don't you have swim after school?"

Shoot. She's right, I do have swim after school. Although I could easily tell them that I am not feeling well, lying has always felt wrong to me. Maybe it's my mother's face every time I've even thought about lying to her face, or maybe it's the fact that I am not good at it, but I just can't lie. Not today. Not when the meet will most likely have scouts from colleges. My parents even promised to be there.

I huff out a deep breath then nod my head at my best friend. We wave goodbye, going our sperate ways, and I head for the girl's locker room to change and speak with my coach.

Today was supposed to be the day.

Chapter 2

My arms run against the water's current, faster and faster my feet kick as I barely hear the roar of the crowd through the echoes of the water, turning louder as I take a breath.

I can feel the other team catching up to me, can my feel my opponent on my right side, but I know enough about this sport to know I am currently ahead. My name is being shouted form everyone on the side and when my hand finally touches the concrete slab and the buzzer goes off, I know that I have won.

I step out of the pool with the help of my teammates and coach and am immediately engulfed by fifteen sets of hands and hugs. I smile, a smile so large I didn't know I owned and peek around at my time.

"Congrats, Gwen," I hear all around me, but only one voice sounds louder than the rest.

"Thanks, coach." My coach, Alison Brennan, was once my babysitter when I was a kid. And when she came back from college, to coach high school swim, I knew that I had to be on her team. After all, she was the one that once taught me how to swim.

I walk over to the opponent, a member of the red devils from Baskin High School in Romeoville. I shake her hand and give her a hug. Lissette Gonzalez was someone I heard great things about. It was an honor to swim against her. I tell her as much and in return and blessed with a wicked smirk.

"Thanks. Great game, Gwen. I've heard a lot about you, too." I blush, then turn away and spot my parents and little brothers in the stands. My dad, as usual, is standing and clapping, well past the typical clap time frame. I give them a small wave, then give my mother the look she is all too familiar with. Seconds later my dad is being pulled back down to his seat.

Back in the locker room, coach is giving us the job well done speech as we are getting dressed. After a few rounds of applause and even more cheesy cheering, we are left alone to finish the rest of our Friday afternoon.

I've been in swim since I was nine years old. I've loved everything about it, but didn't think of joining a team until my junior year. Since then, it's been the only thing on my mind.

Well, almost the only thing.

Earlier thoughts and images flood my head as I think about how stupid I must have looked waiting on Alston to get out of class. I've had a crush on him since I was twelve and knowing now that the only reason, I was asked to meet him was to spread the word to another girl….is heartbreaking.

"Can I get a picture?" I turn and spot Jake, my other best friend of over ten years. His blonde hair and deep green eyes stare at me through a lens as his large frame comes closer.

Jake and I had almost every class together starting in fifth grade and became instant best friends. Adding Nancy to the mix just created a cherry on top. The three of us have always been inseparable and now that the three of us are thinking of going to the same college the mix is getting even better.

Jake is an avid baseball player, always has been and even though his father is a little on the hard side, his passion for always pushing Jake further and further is the reason the dream of getting scouted was recently granted.

"Come on shortie, just one." I place my hand up, covering the lens so that he doesn't get a disgusting picture of me in my swimsuit. Jake adores the photography world, a passion I didn't know he had until this year.

"No way," I giggle, when he pretends to place the camera down, only to snap a picture quickly. Pulling the strap of the camera from around his neck, he turns it off then looks at me with a look of pity. Great. Nancy has already told him about my epic plan failure with Alston. "I take it you heard?"

"Well, if it helps. I had to practically drag it out of Nancy."

I scoff. "Let me guess. That took all of thirteen seconds?"

"Seventeen. New record for her." I roll my eyes and follow him towards the bleachers. I can spot my mother and father attempting to handle my twin seven-year-old brothers. They're both a handful and always give my parents a run for their money but they're loved like no one's business. "Don't matter anyways Gwen, I'm sure someone else would love to go to that pathetic dance with you."

"It's not pathetic."

"That's because you're a hopeless romantic." I cross my arms like I'm offended, but I'm not. Jake is right. I'm a fool for anything romance and he damn well knows it. "Oh, come on, shortie. Think about it. Do you even truly know this Alston prick?"

"Yes."

"No," we say at the same time. "How could you say you know him?"

"I know of him. I know he volunteers at the animal shelter every month."

"That's because he's banging on the receptionist there."

"Eww, Jake."

"It's true." I push him away as I make my way towards my parents. I know if my mother doesn't congratulate me before I make it to the locker room, I will be chased down elsewhere.

"Mom, dad, thanks for coming."

My mom is the first to reach me. Her hands fly around my neck as she brings me into her body with a firm mom hug. I can hear my dad chuckle behind her as he awaits his turn. Once mom allows me a moment of fresh air, I am swarmed by my dad's large frame. The place I've always felt comfortable in. I wasn't always theirs and my story didn't have the perfect beginning of love and protection, but I'm loved now, and that's all I care about.

"Proud of you, baby girl.",

"You did great, Gwen," Charlie shouts, and Owen gives me his typical thumbs up. They may be twins but Owen has always been the more calm and quieter one. Anytime a glass was broken, or a house was bombed with eggs, we knew who the instigator was and who was the one that simply followed.

"Thanks guys." I high five Owen, then turn as I hear my name being called by coach.

"Great meet today, Gwen. Listen, I have a gentleman here to meet you." I turn where she is waving her hand and watch a large older man with a big wad of gray hair, walk towards me. "He's a scout from Stanford and he's heard some amazing things about you. Why don't you go and get dressed and the two of you, along with your parents, can talk."

I nod my head, not wanting my parents to see my reaction. On the outside, I always manage to play cool and collected about my future plans, but the truth is, I don't necessarily have one. Swimming has always been my passion but to be honest, I use it more for earning a scholarship. I'm good, dedicated and passionate for the sport, but it's not something I saw myself doing for the rest of my life.

Not something I necessarily want my parents knowing.

I make my way to the locker-room, and bump right into the person I didn't want to see but knew I would have to.

Joanna Wilder.

The one Alston wants. The one he's been after since I received word that he wanted to meet me after school today.

Her long auburns hair is curled at the tips from swimming. She's an amazing swimmer. She's also avid on the decathlon and the cheerleading team. Her and Alston are simply meant to be. That's what I tell myself as I give her my best impression of a smile.

"Hey, Gwen. Great meet today."

"Thanks." I shrug, then stop her just as she's turning around. I could curse myself for being so pathetic as to actually set these two up, but if rumors got around that I knew Alston wanted to ask her to the Valentine's Day dance I would hate myself. "By the way, Alston wanted me to tell you that he wants to speak with you."

"Alston? Jeffries?"

"That very one." I smile, then look down at the blue tiled wet floor. "I think he wanted to ask you to the Valentine's Day dance."

"Really?" She nearly shouts, and I'm taken back a bit. I could see them together, I think a blind person could, but I never knew they even knew of each other. Where Alston is the bad boy football player, Joanna is more of a sweet little innocent flower. She may be a cheerleader, but she's not exactly the stereotype that follows. She's got her hands dipped in many after school clubs, including the debate team, Culture Club, she's even editor of the school's newspaper.

"Yes. I'm sure he's here somewhere. He knew I had swim with you so...."

"Oh God. Wow. Thanks, Gwen." She turns and springs off before I could blink. My heart hammering fades, and I shake my head and make my way towards my locker, hoping to just put that whole conversation behind me.

I make it to my locker and stop when I spot a pink note tapped to the front. Narrowing my eyes, I look around but no one else has one on their own. Most of the girls are already dressed and wave a hello, followed by a few congratulations as I walk by. I grab the note and flip it over, stunned when I see the message on the other side.

I've loved you since the day you stumbled into my life.
I knew you were the one that I could be with for eternity.
I've wanted to ask you out for a long time, but I was too
chicken.
Not anymore.
Meet me at the Valentine's Day dance tomorrow night at
seven.
-Your Valentine

I turn and spot the last girl walking out the now empty locker room.

Was this meant for me?

Is this some kind of sick joke.

I read the letter over and over again not making sense of any of it.

Someone wants to be my Valentine?

Chapter 3

"And you think it was some kind of sick joke?" I balance my phone between my shoulder blade and my cheek, as I walk into my closet shuffling through the few items that aren't thrown around on the floor. Mom always taught me to be organized with my clothing but for the past half hour, that has gone right out of the window as I look for something to wear for tomorrow night.

"It has to be. Why would anyone leave a note on my locker. Isn't that a bit stalkerish?"

"I don't know I think it's kind of romantic." I roll my eyes and turn when I hear my dad call my name from downstairs.

"If you think it's so romantic, you can go in my place, because there is no way I am going to that dance."

"What do you mean? Aren't you the one that is always talking about some guy sweeping you off your feet in exactly these types of ways? You're supposed to be the romantic one here, Gwen. Not me."

"Nancy, if I go, then I'll be walking right into a trap. This is obviously some kind of dumb joke, and I don't want to go alone, then wind up being embarrassed. It's bad enough Alston and Joanna will be there. Together."

"Just please think about it. I have to be there to cover yearbook so we can always hang out if your mystery man is a complete dud." I cringe when I hear my father call my name once more.

"Alright fine, I'll think about it. Listen I have to go, dad is calling me and I'm fairly sure he and mom are wanting to talk about the scholarship offer I got today."

"Got it. See you tomorrow night." Another roll of my eyes and I hang up on her laughing her ass off in the background.

I make my way downstairs and stop when I see Jake in the middle of my kitchen wresting around with Owen and Charlie.

"What are you doing here?" A large smile graces his face when he moves his eyes up towards me.

"Thought I'd come by and tell you congrats on the offer in person. Your dad called my dad." I look behind me at my father and mother sitting on the couch in their usual stance. My dad's protective arm around my mother's small frame.

Dad and Mr. Kennedy have been friends a long time. Mr. Kennedy was one of the first people to take a chance on dad and uncle Sean's business and now even works with them as a business consultant. Dad and mom were proud that I was able to get into Stanford with a full ride.

"You wouldn't happen to hear any news about going to a certain school as well, would you?" I'm baiting him, something he immediately catches up on. He blushes, I knew he would, then places Owen down from his back and walks over to me.

"I got in." I jump into his arms and scream. I can hear my mom giggle and stand up to get some refreshments. Forever the hostess that one.

"When did you find out?"

"A few days ago."

"What?" I jump off him and give him a discerning look.

Stanford was the school Nancy, Jake and I always wanted to get into. Although, it's far from our family, it had everything we each wanted. An amazing athletics department and great art programs. Jake and I would get in with scholarships and Nancy's fancy lawyers of parents would pay for her to get in so that she could continue to express herself in art and business.

"Why didn't you tell me?"

"I wanted to wait for you."

"But you didn't know I would get in. Why would you push down your own happiness." I take his hand in mine and look up at his him. "Jake, even if I didn't get in. I would have been happy for you."

"Well now we can be happy together." He smirks and I throw a punch and land it right into his arm. Dad calls out my name like he always does when I do this very same thing for the past ten years.

"It's his throwing arm, baby girl."

I roll my eyes and laugh when Jake chuckles and acts injured as he makes his way to my mother for a slice of cake. She always seems to have those on hand in this house. Jake is the school's baseball pitcher. He, like me, love sports but it was never something we strived for doing for the rest of our lives. His love for photography and my love for design is where we will end up steering towards once we are in Stanford. *Together.* Just knowing I will have my two best friends by my side on my new journey in a few months is heartwarming.

"So, what's the plan for tomorrow night?"

I turn and watch as my mother gives, the boys a slice of cake each, patting them on their heads when they start complaining about who has the bigger slice. Dad swoops in and evens them out by eating a bit of both.

"Are you talking about the Valentine's Day dance?" Jake asks, then looks over to me with a look I can't quite decipher.

"Yes. Are you two excited to go?"

"Oh, mom please. Jake and I are not going." I roll my eyes, but stop when I notice Jake isn't backing me up. I look over at him and see that he's.... wait is he blushing? "Right?"

"I actually am."

"For yearbook?" Both Jake and Nancy have yearbook this year. They knew it would look good for college applications and that way Jake was able to do something he hides from other people. Photography. He's exceptionally good at it and has always had a passion for it, but to everyone else he's the baseball guy. He, like me, don't want to let on that the sport is only for show.

"No."

"No?" My voice must be louder than I thought because mom shoots dad a look and they both take the boys in the living room to watch How to Train Your Dragon for the millionth time this week. "What do you mean? You asked someone to go?"

"Is that so hard to believe?" he chuckles, then walks over and grabs my not empty plate from my hands. He starts washing and I take my normal place beside him and dry.

"I-I just can't see you asking someone to a school dance." I shrug, but on the inside I'm a little fired up. Jake has dated before, and although none of those girls were even close to good enough for him, he's never been with them long enough to even get as far as he is right now with this mystery woman.

Why the hell am I so angry?

"You should go," he states, and it's enough to snap me back into reality.

"Yeah. Let me show up just in time to be the butt of someone's joke."

"Doubt anyone will be playing you for a fool, Gwen."

"Oh, and why is that?"

"Because you have me." The soap spuds cling to his hands as he passes me the last dish. I stare at his face, not knowing how exactly to respond.

"Jake…"

He stands at full height blessing me with one of his large smiles that he quickly tries to hide. "Just come tomorrow night Gwen. I think you'll be pleasantly surprised." After drying his hands, Jake walks over and kisses me on my forehead, something he always does whenever he is going to leave.

I walk him out as he waves a final goodbye to my little brothers, and stand out on my porch as he hops into his car and drives off.

"Jake going home?" Mom's voice snaps me out of my daze, and I turn to see her coming outside with two cups of what look and smell like hot cocoa.

"Yes. You just missed him."

"It's freezing outside tonight."

"But it feels amazing." In typical mom tradition, she grabs a nearby throw blanket that we keep on the porch swing and sits down patting the seat beside her. I squeeze in and the two of us cuddle inside the blanket with our cocoa. "Where's dad?"

"Putting the two hellions to bed."

"And he doesn't need help?"

"Oh, I'm sure he does. But where's the fun in that."

The two of us laugh as we listen to the sounds of my father wrestling both boys into coercion.

"So, Jake stopped by to congratulate you?"

"Yes. He heard about Stanford and wanted to come by."

"And now the two of you can go to college together."

"Nancy, too."

106

She swings one leg making the swing move back and forth while I place both legs up and cross them. I shut my eyes as I remember the many times we have been in this very position. I've always adored my mother. Everything about her I've loved. Her spirit, her courage, her beauty, even the small bits she displays when she's hurting but trying to remain strong enough for the family. I admire everything about her.

But I would be a fool if I said I didn't think of my real mother here and there. I've wondered about her, and now that I am older, I want to know more about her. I haven't told anyone about my feelings and thoughts, not even Nancy, but lately I've thought of opening up to the one person that can help me. The only one I have left that ever truly knew her.

"So, have you thought of whether or not you're going to go to this Valentine's Day dance?"

I shake my head before I speak. "No. I don't know who left that note on my swim locker, but I'm sure it was either meant for someone else, or it's some kind of dumb prank."

"I think you should." I turn my head and give my mom a 'you're joking, right?' look. "Look, I know the whole note on a locker isn't the most …expecting thing in your generation, but if you never take a chance, then you're setting yourself up for failure."

"Mom, there isn't anyone else that I like. Even if that note were some guy that has always liked me, the only person I wanted was Alston. And I'm sure he's pretty happy right now with Joanna," I try and say her name normal but I' fairly sure it came off petty.

"What was so special about this Alston boy anyways? I mean, don't get me wrong I've seen the kid, and handsome doesn't quite do him justice."

"Gross." I shake my head, laughing and shove her shoulder.

"But can you honestly tell me that you could have seen yourself with him?"

"Yes."

"So, tell me about him. What sort of things is he into?"

"I don't know. Sports and cars?"

"Are you asking me or telling me."

"I'm sure he's into the same things as every other guy. He's a football player, a good one. He's a smart student and he has a nice car." I shrug. Wow, do I really not know things about Alston? I've had a crush on him for as long as I can remember, but I feel like most of that has been superficial. He's handsome, the first boy I ever noticed that was, but I don't think before today, we have ever even said ten words to each other.

"Gwen," she begins, as her hand comes down atop of mine. I turn and watch her eyes turn soft; the same way they do every time she looks at my dad. "Being with someone has to feel special at *all* times. It needs to feel like you found your other half even though you weren't aware you weren't whole. You need to make sure you always feel important and cherished and loved. So, go to that dance, go and have fun and dance with your friends, and if there is someone special that sees *you* as something special, then hold on and never let go."

I stare at my mother for what feels like hours. It isn't until my dad comes out to check on us, one kid strapped to each leg, does my mother stand to help him bathe and put my little brothers to bed. Just as she steps into the house, I stop her by calling her name.

"How did you know dad was the one?"

"He told me." She winks then turns and walks inside.

Chapter 4

I turn once more as I look myself up and down in the full-size mirror. It took some persuasion and the promise of a vast amount of baked goods from mom if this night turns out terrible, but I am officially going to the Valentine's Day dance.

"You look beautiful." I smile as I look down at the reflection of Owen. Turning around I giggle when I see his attempt at placing on one of dad's ties around his neck.

Owen has always been a little romantic. He always asks dad questions about love and marriage. Although only eight, the kid has the soul of someone ten times his age.

"Thanks kiddo." I smile then turn around and look myself up and down once again.

I've decided to go with a typical little black dress. It has a lace front and flares at the bottom, stopping just above my knee. I've paired it with red heels and red earrings and mom was able to have Aunt Gina come by and style my hair into a messy bun. I feel nice but can't exactly stop the worrying pit of doom from lurking through the shadows.

"Gwen. Time to go hun." I wink at my brother when he cat calls as I move towards the door and down the stairs. Dad, Uncle Sean, Aunt Gina, mom, and Charles all stand around as I make my way downstairs as if I were some fair maiden being sold for a heard of chickens.

"Wait, you're wearing that?" Dad is the first to stand and walk over, grabbing a nearby blanket and attempting to cover me up. Aunt Gina comes to my rescue quickly swatting him in the arm.

"Oh no you don't Brandon. I worked hard on her hair. Besides, it's a special night for her," she laughs then winks.

Rolling my eyes, I look over at mom who simply shrugs. Of course, mom and dad have told Uncle Sean and Aunt Gina about my mystery date. That doesn't make me seem desperate and lame at all. Cue another eye roll.

"Mom, dad, can I have the last cookie?" Serena comes storming out crashing right into the sofa. Uncle Sean picks up his daughter and laughs as she attempts to fix her hair.

"Didn't you already have like ten cookies kid?"

"Nooooo," she states, and none of us are shocked to see Uncle Sean immediately giving into his nine-year-old princess. Serena was the only child they had because of unfortunate circumstances regarding them trying again, but she's loved fiercely and spoiled rottenly.

"So, is he going to pick you up or are you meeting him there?" Mom asks, as she comes over and hands me my coat and purse.

"Good question. Nothing else was on the note, so I'll drive there, stand in the middle of the dance floor and hope my mystery man even knows what I look like. Don't freak when I come home covered in tar and feathers." I narrow my eyes at my mother only to roll them when Charles begins asking questions about feathers and tar to my dad.

"Don't worry honey. I think you'll be pleasantly surprised by whatever the night will bring you." I give her a kiss on her cheek, followed by my dad who has a list of rules regarding meeting a mystery boy and how he wouldn't look good in an orange jumpsuit, and within minutes I'm out of the door.

The entire eleven minutes it takes me to get to the school, I have talked myself into about ten different scenarios. I've thought of just turning the car around more times than I can count, but one thing keeps me rooted in the seat. One thing tells me that this night doesn't have to be a compete bust.

My friends.

Knowing Nancy and Jake are here is a comforting feeling. I park, then walk into the dance, smiling at the cheesy, yet warming background of the night. There are heart shaped balloons everywhere. Pink, white and red streamers are strown about. A large heart shaped cardboard cutout with our school's name on it greets me as I walk further inside to see the dance has already gotten started.

More students showed up than I would have thought, and I catch Nancy and her boyfriend Manuel on the dance floor getting their bodies reacquainted with each other. Walking further into the room, I 'm relieved when she spots me and practically drags Manuel towards me.

"You made it!" she shouts over the music. I nod my head with a smile on my face then hug her boyfriend. Manuel is Nancy's everything. He's kind and extremely smart. Although, they did not get into the same school for college, they are willing to make it work.

"Mom talked me into coming. I wasn't going to, but knowing you and Jake are here made me feel a little more confident."

"Jake?" she asks, giving me a confused look. "Jake's not here."

"What?"

"Well, he was, then he left with that one chick with the Romanian accent." Both Nancy and I look over at Manuel. "What? Isn't she Romanian?"

I roll my eyes and then cross my arms. Picturing Jake with that desperately seeking attention Sonia makes my skin crawl. Does he not understand he can do so much better?

"Listen, I don't want you to feel weird, but I got a letter form that secret admirer guy. It says that he wants you to meet him outside at the gazebo."

"What? You got a letter from him? Who is he?" Does she not understand how strange that is?

"I have no idea, Gwen. It was on my car's windshield when I went to make a call to my mom outside." She digs around in her purse and finds the note. "I think he figured you and I would drive together."

Meet me at the Gazebo at 8pm sharp.
-Your Valentine

I reread I once more before folding it and placing it in my black bag. Nancy's eyes are sparkling, making my typical eye roll come out.

"Gwen, are you seriously going to tell me you don't want to know who this is?"

"That's right. I have no plan on going to some darkened hideout and being hit with sand or silly string or something."

"What if this guy really is the one?"

"I think you've been reading too many of my romance books," Nancy huffs out a breath, crossing her arms like a toddler.

"Alright that's enough babe. Come on, let's boogie some more." I smirk at her when Manuel shakes his head with laughter, then takes her hand and leads her back to the dance floor.

I make my way back towards the front of the building ready to head home, but stop when I see Joanna and Alston. Joanna spots me immediately and I cringe when she waves me over.

"Hey Gwen. Listen, I heard what you did for me and Alston. I wanted to thank you."

Her perfectly manicured hands rest on his bicep as he talks with someone from the football team. He's wearing a tux with a tie matching her pale pink dress completely. Yuck.

"No problem. I'm glad I could play matchmaker for you two." She bypasses my dry condescending tone and instead, nearly knocks me over with her next words.

"Can you believe that Sonia Bareli? I mean, she had a date, then totally left with that older kid that was pushed back like twice."

"What?" My heart pounds wildly in my chest. Sonia? That's who Nancy said was Jake's date.

"Yeah, she had a date, but the poor guy was turned away when she left with someone else. Last I saw of her, she was lip locking with him in the bathroom."

Rage burns my vision as I thank them then make my way towards the Gazebo. The sooner I meet this jerk that wants to play a game with me, the sooner I can get to Jake's house and talk with him. He's never really shown interest in other girls and Sonia isn't exactly his type, but knowing that he is somewhere hurting because of her is making me see red.

Lights illuminate the small white gazebo. It was a gift from our senior class to the agriculture department's lead Miss Rodriguez. She was shot trying to save a mentally ill student and although she made it, she is now wheelchair bound. Our class decided on a gazebo as our parting gift knowing she would love to sit and watch her students.

As I make my way to the inside, I spot rose petals strown about followed by many candles. I'm almost hypnotized by the shadows of the flames dancing around the lights illuminating the whole thing.

It's magical.

"Figured you'd like it." A small bluish covers my body as every small puzzle piece fit into place. I turn and beam as my eyes lock on Jake.

"Jake." His name is a whisper, not one I've said before, but one that feels good.

"I know you're pissed at me for doing this to you," he states, with his hands held high in surrender. "But I had to tell you in a way that would rock you."

"Why?" Another whisper. This boy has gotten me whispering.

"You know why, Gwen." Do I? I do. I've always loved and cared for Jake. Many people would say that they always thought we would end up together because of close we were. He knows me better than I know myself and as he moves closer, his black tux showing off his large frame, he's who I always knew he would be.

Someone special.

"Jake, why didn't you just tell me? This is amazing, don't get me wrong, but why didn't you just come to me?"

"Because I know you, Gwen." He stops just before reaching me and holds his hand out for me to grab. I do so, my body shaking as he takes me into the gazebo and sits me down. My eyes are trained on him but his are on our hands that have yet to part. "I knew you would fight this. Fight what I've always known and hoped would happen. I don't want to fight the way I feel anymore."

"Were my parents and Nancy in on this?"

"Yeah," he chuckles, then shakes his head. God how I want to run my hands through his hair. "They always knew what I did, but knew I was too chicken shit to tell you. Like I said, I'm done waiting. I had to make a pretend date to get here, but Sonia knew what I had planned and made plans for herself with another guy."

"What made you change your mind?" Why am I asking him all these questions? On the inside, I'm fuming, I cannot believe this is happening, but I want to be safe, want to be sure. I have to be. Because unlike any other guy, I can't lose Jake.

"You were so excited about that Alston dick. I didn't want to lose you to anyone, I knew I had to make my move, especially when I got accepted into Stanford." His hands grip mine tighter and he finally brings his gaze towards me. The green in his eyes is even brighter than normal, something I find myself getting lost in. "I want to be with you, Gwen. I've wanted you for years and as much as this may be scaring you, I've never been more sure of anything in my life."

My heart is beating so fast and loudly I feel as if it will burst out of my skin at any moment. My chest is constricting, and my breathing is rapid, yet none of those things feel like a bad thing. I've got butterflies in my stomach and a large smile plastered on my face. A giggle burst free and I cover my mouth with my hands only to have them be pushed back down my Jake.

"I take that as a yes?"

Is it a yes? Am I really sure I want to try this with Jake. My soul Is telling me to do it, to take a chance, the same way Jake is. I don't want to ruin our friendship, but I won't stand here and lie to him either. "I've always loved you, too, Jake. I've always wanted you but when our friendship became stronger, I knew I couldn't risk losing you."

"Then take a chance baby. Take a chance on us."

Baby. He called me baby.

Every single doubt I had in my head flurries out of the door and I find myself leaning into him enveloping his scent. The moment my lips connect with his, I know I can never push away the feelings I have for him. The ones I always have.

I love Jake Kennedy. I always have, and right now I'm ready to give it all a chance. He's my very own Valentine.

Kayleigh's Valentine

Surprise

A Bay State University Novel

Short Story

by

Katie Holland

Chapter 1

Major

I was pacing the length of the main living area in our dorm. I had to ask Bodie something, but I wasn't sure how he was going to react.

"Dude," Bodie said to me, "chill the fuck out and tell me what's going on."

"So, it's Valentine's Day," I finally said.

"Yeah, I know … and?"

"Well, I have this whole night planned for Kayleigh. I want to make it really special and something she'll never forget."

"Okay … just spit it out already."

"I need you to stay with Karma at the girl's dorm tonight," I blurted out.

Bodie looked at me like I'd lost my mind, and I really didn't blame him. I knew things were more than a little weird between him and Karma right now, but I'd needed to ask him.

"Uh … what?"

"I would take Kayleigh to a hotel, but she has to be at practice at six tomorrow morning and I thought it would be better if we were on campus, so she didn't have to get up extra early."

"And you just decided to ask me this today, like a few hours before your date?"

"Sorry man, I was going to ask you last week, but then the shit hit the fan with Karma, so I waited until that calmed down a little."

"What does Karma think about this?"

"Kayleigh is waiting to ask her until she hears from me."

"You know you're a dick, right?"

"I know, but I'm only asking because I want Kayleigh to have the night of her life."

Bodie sighed. "Fine. If Karma's okay with it then I'll do it, but you owe me."

"Thanks, man."

"Whatever. What time is your date?"

"I'm picking Kayleigh up at seven. I guess you and Karma can work out the details on your end."

"Just let me know what she says."

I nodded and pulled out my phone to text Kayleigh.

Me: Bodie said he'd stay with Karma tonight
Kayleigh: Ok, I'll run it by Karma

I waited a few minutes for her to talk to Karma. I didn't realize how nervous I was until I jumped when my phone dinged.

Kayleigh: She's ok with it.
Me: Great, I'll see you at 7

"Hey, Bodie," I called out to him, "Karma's okay with you staying there."

"Awesome." I could hear the sarcasm in his voice from the other room.

Now that that was settled, there was a lot that had to be done in the next few hours. I started making calls to a whole lot of people to finalize the details for the night. It was times like this that my money came in really handy. It was amazing what you could get done last minute if you had money to back you up.

An hour before I was picking Kayleigh up, I jumped in the shower. After I dried off, I put on her favorite cologne and got ready. I was going all out tonight so I put on my dark grey suit with a black dress shirt. I decided to not wear the tie I'd picked out, so I left the top button undone. She'd mentioned once that she loved it when just the top button of my shirt was undone, and I wanted to drive her as crazy as I knew she was going to drive me.

I slipped her gift into my pocket, and with one last look in the mirror, I was good to go.

"I'm going to head over to the girls' place," I told Bodie, when I walked out of my room.

"I'll come with you," he said. "Karma told me to just come over when you pick up Kayleigh and we'll order some food."

I nodded and grabbed my keys. I was both nervous and excited as we left the dorm. I wanted the night to be as perfect as I could possibly make it, and honestly, I just really wanted to put a million smiles on Kayleigh's face. Here's hoping I didn't forget anything.

Chapter 2

Kayleigh

"You look absolutely gorgeous," Karma told me. "And totally hot, too."

I smiled at her. "Thanks to you."

Taking another look in the mirror, my smile grew bigger. Karma had done an excellent job on my hair and makeup. My hair was often in a ponytail and I hardly ever wore any makeup, but tonight I felt like a movie star.

The black dress I borrowed from Karma fit me perfectly. It had a fairly low neckline, was tight at the waist and flowed down to my knees. She'd paired it with silver strappy heels and bracelets that matched the shoes. I wondered if Major was even going to recognize me. A text alert on my phone got my attention.

Major: I'm thinking dirty thoughts about you.
I giggled.
Me: Wait until you see what I'm wearing.
Major: Now I want to get you naked twice as bad.

"You're blushing," Karma said, grinning. "Is Major text fucking you again?"

"A little," I admitted.

"Good, you've come a long way but there's still room for improvement."

She was smiling at me, so I knew she was kidding, but she was also right. At the start of the year, I was sexually inexperienced and not good with guys, but Major had brought out the side of me that I'd been wanting to set free. After I'd asked Major to help me, we'd spent hours texting each other. Most of it was sexual, but not all of it. When his texts became the best part of my day, I realized I was falling for him. That hadn't been part of the plan, but lucky for me it turned out he felt the same.

"Kayleigh," Karma said, snapping her fingers in my face. "Are you still with me?"

"Huh?"

She shook her head at me. "One text from Major and you turn into a zombie. I'm never going to let that happen to me."

"But what about Anthony?"

"What about him?"

"You don't see yourself falling in love with him?"

"I'm not sure I'll ever be in love and I'm totally fine with that."

I shook my head at her. I knew she'd fall hard for someone and I was going to be there to witness it.

"Anyway," she said, "it's almost seven. Are you ready for your hot date?"

I couldn't stop the grin from forming on my face. I had no idea what Major had planned but I was really looking forward to it.

"I'm soooo ready."

"He's going to go crazy when he sees what you've got on under that dress."

"I hope so."

There was a knock on the door.

"Show time," Karma said and answered the door.

The look on Major's face when he saw me was worth the hour of getting ready. I watched as his eyes started at my face then did a sweep of my body. He also had that look he gave me when he was thinking really dirty thoughts.

"Calm down there, lover boy," Karma said. "I don't need to see those thoughts on your face. Save it until you two are alone. Now, go on and have a good time."

I walked over to Major and took his hand. "You look very handsome tonight."

"And I don't even have words for how beautiful you look."

I know I was grinning like an idiot. "Thank you."

"Are you ready?" he asked.

I nodded and he led me out of the dorm room.

"When we got in the elevator, I turned to face him. "Are you going to tell me where we're going yet?"

He grinned. "Not yet, but you're going to love it."

"Whatever it is, I'm sure it's going to be great," I told him, and kissed his cheek.

Chapter 3

Major

There were a million thoughts running through my head, but the one that overruled them all was how sexy Kayleigh looked. If no one had been around I would have stripped her in the dorm and fucked her on the couch, but that part of the plan came later.

When the elevator dinged, I grabbed her hand and led her outside. The limo pulled up just in time. The driver got out and came around to open the door.

"You got us a limo?" The smile on her face was worth it.

"Only the best for you," I told her. "After you."

I helped her get into the limo and climbed in after her. The driver shut the door and a minute later we were moving.

Just as I'd asked, there was champagne chilling on ice and two long stem glasses. I popped the cork and poured us each a glass.

"I know you don't drink," I said, as I handed her a glass, "but tonight is special and I wanted to make a toast, so you only have to have a sip if you want."

"Okay."

As I turned to face her our knees touched. I could feel the heat of her skin through my pants and of course my thoughts went back to getting her naked.

"Major?" she asked.

"Huh?"

"You're just staring at me."

"Oh," I chuckled. "Sorry, I was thinking those dirty thoughts about you again."

The blush that appeared on her cheeks was one of the things I loved about her. The combination of sexy and shy was something I didn't know turned me on until I met her.

"Back to my toast." I gathered my thoughts for a minute before continuing. "Kayleigh, since the first day we met on the beach, there hasn't been a day that's gone by that I haven't thought about you. It took me a long time to admit that, but I'm really glad I did. So, here's to accidental meetings and beaches."

She grinned as we clinked glasses. "I thought about you, too, even though I tried really hard not to at first. Asking you to help me become more comfortable with sexual things was the best decision I've ever made. So, here's to good decisions and texting."

I smiled back at her and we clinked glasses again.

A few minutes later, the limo stopped, and the driver opened our door. I made sure I got out first so I could see the look on her face when she figured out where we were. As I helped her out, I watched as she realized where I'd brought her. The smile that lit up her face made my heart jump.

"Major, this is the beach where we first met. I didn't know you could be this romantic."

"And this is just the start of the night. The best is yet to come."

I took her hand and we started walking towards the beach. The party planning company I'd hired had done everything I'd asked. We walked on a temporary boardwalk to a tent that was lit up with white lights and flowers were everywhere.

Kayleigh hadn't stopped smiling since we got out of the limo and I hoped she stayed that way all night.

"Major, this is just beautiful. It's like we're in our own little world here."

There was soft music playing and the lights gave off enough light to create the romantic feel I'd wanted. They'd even used some kind of sheer curtain on the inside of the tent to make it feel more like a room and less like a tent. They were definitely getting a big tip from me.

I pulled out the chair for Kayleigh, then sat down across from her. The candle on the table was making her eyes sparkle.

"This is like a dream," she said as she took my hand in hers. "I can't believe you did all of this for me."

"I'd do anything for you." And I really meant it.

The front of the tent was open to the ocean and I watched as Kayleigh stared out at it. I grinned when she realized the significance of the spot we were sitting in.

"Is this really the exact place Karma and I were lying in the sun when you guys came over to talk to us?"

"Yes," I grinned. "Who knew that a stuck-up brunette would become the most important thing in my life."

She giggled. "And who knew that an arrogant player would become the most important thing in mine."

I winked at her. "Just goes to show you that first impressions aren't always right."

She smiled. "Very true."

Chapter 4

Kayleigh

The night had only just started, and it was like I was living a fantasy. I couldn't believe that Major had come up with this as our Valentine's date. It was way over the top, but I was loving every second of it. I'd never felt more special than I did right then.

I watched as a man in a suit entered the tent. "May I offer you something to drink?"

"Yes please, I'll just have water with lemon if that's okay."

"Of course, miss. And for the gentleman?"

"Water is fine for me, too," Major told him.

He was back a minute later with two wine glasses. He set them down in front of us. "Dinner will be served shortly," he said and left the tent.

"This still doesn't seem real," I told Major. "I've never experienced anything like this before."

"I wanted to make our first Valentine's something you'd remember forever."

"I think you've accomplished that. This is the most romantic thing I've ever heard of someone doing. You get lots of bonus points for this one."

He chuckled. "I wasn't going for bonus points, but I'll take them. I just wanted you to have some idea of what you mean to me." Then he chuckled again. "Never in a million years did I think I would ever say something like that."

I grinned at that. "You've come a long way since that first day on the beach."

"So, have you, Kayleigh."

"Thanks to you."

"You did all the work, I just nudged you in the right direction."

I laughed. "You did a lot more than nudge me."

Major grinned. "Yeah, I did, but it was so much fun making you blush, even when I wasn't there with you."

"I still haven't quite gotten over that part yet."

"And I hope you never do. I love seeing you blush because of me."

Major was about to say something when the man in the suit came back with our dinner. He set down a plate in front of me that looked like it should be served in a restaurant that had a year long waiting list.

"Wow, Major, this looks amazing. Where is it from?"

"One of mom's friends has a personal chef, so I asked if she could make us a special meal."

"It smells delicious, but what is it exactly?"

He laughed. "All I know is that I asked for something that was healthy and tasted great."

"Okay, then let's try it."

After taking my first bite I knew I was going to eat everything on my plate. It turned out to be some kind of chicken with roasted veggies and a salad, but that description didn't do it justice. Each bite was bursting with flavor, even the salad.

"I think I want a personal chef for my birthday," I said, with a laugh.

"Done," Major said, and grinned at me.

After our plates were cleared, we were brought dessert. I just stared at what was in front of me. It was a tiny three-layer cake. The bottom layer was covered in shiny chocolate, and the middle one had extremely intricate scrollwork done in frosting, but it was the top one that really got my attention. It was covered in gold.

"Is that real gold?" I asked, as I took a closer look.

"Probably."

"And you can eat it?"

Major laughed at me. "I don't think we'd be served something we couldn't eat."

"I need a picture of this," I told him.

He pulled out his phone and took several pictures for me.

"Are you just going to look at it or are you going to try it?" he teased me.

"I don't know. I might be too pretty to eat."

"Not for me," he said, and dug into the cake. "Mmm, this is so good, Kayleigh. If you don't at least try it, I'm going to eat yours too."

I wasn't about to let that happen, so I took a bite. "Is this chef magic or something? This is the best cake I've ever had."

Major grinned. "And this isn't even the best part of the night."

Despite the fact I'd probably have to do extra laps in the pool tomorrow I ate every bit of my dessert, even the gold.

"Thank you Major," I told him when we were both finished. "This has been the best night."

"Anything for you Kayleigh. Now it's time for your gift."

Chapter 5

Major

I was a little nervous about what I was about to give Kayleigh. My hope was to show her what she meant to me without going over the top.

"So," I started, "I think I need to say a few things before I give you what's in my pocket. First of all, until you came along, I didn't know what it was like to care more about someone other than myself. When I realized that I was in love with you, I really didn't know what to do. But the more I said it to myself, the more I knew it was right. And when you went missing, I thought I was going to go out of my mind until we found you. I'd never been so scared in my life. I knew then that you were the most important thing in the world to me." I took the small black box out of my pocket and put it in Kayleigh's hands. She opened it and saw the ring I'd picked out for her. It was a simple platinum band with pink diamonds in it. "I know we're still young, and I'm not asking you to marry me … yet, but I want this to represent what you mean to me and that I know you're always going to be part of my future."

I watched as the first tear slid down her cheek, but the smile on her face could light up a room.

"Major, I love it and I love the thought behind it. I had no idea you could be so romantic."

"I'm just full of surprises, but I'm still thinking about getting you naked."

That made her laugh, just like I'd hoped.

"This really is a beautiful ring. I'll be proud to wear it. What finger does it go on?"

"I was hoping it would fit on your right ring finger. Kinda like practice for later." I winked at her.

She smiled and slid it on the finger I suggested. It was a perfect fit. The jeweler would definitely be getting more of my business.

"I got something for you, too," she said. "But it's not quite on the level of what you gave me."

"I know I'll love it no matter what," I told her, and I meant it.

Kayleigh reached in her purse and pulled out a box that wasn't much bigger than the one I'd given her. "Here," she said, and put it in my hand.

When I opened the box, I grinned. It was the perfect gift for me. She'd gotten me a leather necklace with a small metal surfboard wrapped in wire.

"Since surfing was the reason we started spending time together, I thought it was a good gift for you. It's also handmade in Hawaii."

"You couldn't have gotten me anything better. I love it, Kayleigh, and I can't wait to show it off."

The smile on her face made my heart beat faster, and my dick twitch in my pants.

"I think it's time to get out of here," I whispered. "Are you ready?"

She nodded.

"Then let's go." I grabbed her hand, and we ran back to the limo.

Chapter 6

Kayleigh

The second we got in the limo and it started moving the air seemed to be charged with electricity.

Major turned to look at me. "I think we need to experience another first."

I was sure I knew what he had in mind but decided to play along. "And what might that be?"

"My mouth on that sweet pussy."

I knew I blushed, but I also squeezed my legs together at the thought.

"I can tell you'd like that as much as me."

He slid over beside me and I smiled as his hand went under my dress. I was waiting for him to discover my surprise for him. I grinned at the look on his face when he found it.

"Fuck, Kayleigh. You're not wearing any panties."

"Nope. Happy Valentine's Day."

"It's a good thing I didn't know that earlier, or I might have bent you over the table at the beach."

I giggled. "I wanted it to be a surprise."

"I'm surprised alright. Now I get to have some fun."

Major got down on my knees in front of me and lifted the dress, so it was out of his way. I opened my legs automatically because I loved what I knew was coming. With the first swipe of his tongue, I moaned.

"The driver," I managed to say.

"Don't worry I would never let anyone but me see you like this, but he might hear you so that part's up to you."

When his tongue licked me again, I put my hand over my mouth. Major had a lot of skills and this was definitely one of them. His tongue circled my clit and when he sucked on it, I yelped at little.

He chuckled, but never took his tongue off me. In only a few minutes, he had me squirming in the seat. I watched his head between my legs and for some reason the fact that we were still fully dressed was extra hot.

"I love that you're so wet for me, Kayleigh. You're so fucking sexy."

I was going to say something back, but the words left my mouth when his tongue entered me, and his thumb found my clit. All I could manage was moaning. My fingers found his hair and I held him in place. I could feel him smile against me, but he didn't stop.

The pleasure was building, and I knew it was going to be intense when it happened. Major moved his tongue back to my clit and slid two fingers in me. That pushed me over the edge. I came, panting his name and melted into a puddle.

When I was able to open my eyes, I saw Major with a huge grin on his face.

"You look very pleased with yourself," I told him.

"I am."

"You should be. That was amazing," I said, noticing he had to adjust himself.

I giggled. "I think you need some help with that." I pointed to his obvious hardon.

"We'll be taking care of that very soon."

"We're stopped. Where are we?"

"Back on campus. I wanted to take you to a hotel but knowing you had practice in the morning I thought it would be better if you were closer to home."

"You're so sweet."

He laughed. "I'm definitely not thinking sweet thoughts right now. It's time to get you upstairs." He took my hand and slid me over to him.

The night had already been perfect, I couldn't imagine what he could do to top it.

Chapter 7

Major

Luckily, the suit jacket I had on covered the front of my pants. I was so hard it almost hurt and knowing Kayleigh was walking through the building without any panties on was driving me crazy. It was torture while we waited for the elevator and when we finally got on it, we weren't alone. I could see the grin on Kayleigh's face, and I was sure she knew what I was thinking.

When we finally got to my dorm room, I unlocked the door and let her walk in first. I wanted her to be as surprised as she was earlier.

"Oh Major," she whispered, "this is just amazing. You did all this for me?"

"Of course, I did."

While Kayleigh and I had been at the beach, I'd had the same company that set up the romantic dinner transform the dorm room. The whole room was filled with flickering candles, vases of flowers and soft music playing in the background, but the best part was the look on her face.

I used to use my money on all kinds of stupid shit, but now it was all about Kayleigh. If I could make her happy, I was going to do it.

"I feel so spoiled," she said, as she looked around the room again.

"Get used to it," I told her, "because I'm going to do it as often as I can."

She grinned and I'm pretty sure I saw a tear in her eye, but I knew it was a happy tear.

Kayleigh moved so that she was standing in front of me. "It's time to unwrap the rest of your present."

She turned around and waited. It took me a second to figure out what she wanted. I grinned when I realized I was supposed to undress her. I was totally on board with that plan, but I had a few ideas of my own.

Sliding her hair over her right shoulder I kissed her skin right above where her zipper started, and for every inch that I pulled her zipper down I kissed her again. When I'd gotten her dress halfway undone, I stopped.

"You're not wearing a bra either? Are you trying to kill me?"

She giggled. "Surprise."

All thoughts of going slow went right out of my head. Knowing she'd been naked under her dress all night made me a little crazy. A few seconds later, I had her dress all the way off. I scooped her up in my arms and carried her to my bedroom.

Kayleigh was grinning when I put her down on the bed. "I kind of like this side of you."

"You mean crazed sex maniac?"

She laughed. "Yeah."

"Well then get ready to hang on," I told her.

I practically ripped my suit off and when I couldn't get the buttons of my shirt undone, I tore it off over my head. When I finally got naked, I grabbed a condom and put it on. Crawling on to the bed I moved so that my entire body was over top of her.

Sliding my hand over her chest and down to her pussy, my fingers found her clit. "You have no idea how much it turns me on that you're so wet for me," I whispered. "Now I'm going to slide my dick in you and make you scream."

The look on her face was enough to tell me she was ready. I moved so that I was at her entrance and as I slowly slid in, I think it was torturing me more than her.

"Please Major, I don't think I can take slow right now," she said, and opened her legs wider for me.

I knew exactly how she felt. We'd been building to this all night and now it was finally here.

Chapter 8

Kayleigh

Major was either trying to drive me crazy or kill me with the slow torturous way he was entering me. Not wearing any underwear all night had turned me on more than I thought, so I was more than ready for him.

When he was finally all the way in me, he stilled, but only for a second, then he started sliding in and out of me.

"That feels amazing," I breathed.

My first experiences with sex were less than stellar, but everything with Major was so much more than I could have thought possible. I always felt so connected to him when we were together.

Something he taught me about myself was that I loved watching him while we were having sex. I loved the way his muscles flexed, the look of pleasure on his face and most of all, I loved seeing his dick move in and out of me.

He caught me watching and grinned. "My naughty girl, but now it's my turn to watch."

Major slid out of me and we switched places. I eased down on him, put my hands on his chest and it was my turn to move.

"I love you like this," he told me. "You are so beautiful and sexy and all mine."

He moved his hand to my chest and gently pinched my nipples. I pinched his nipples back and he moaned. I smiled and started to move my body up and down. The feel of his hands as he touched me sent little shivers all over me, but I needed more.

"I need you," I told him.

He understood what I meant and flipped us back over. When he sunk into me, we both moaned. This time there was no holding back, for either of us.

"Yes Major, just like that. I love the way you make me feel."

"Is that the best you've got?" he teased.

I had to smile at that. "Fuck me like you mean it, Major."

"Better," he said, and started pounding into me.

Anything else I had to say was forgotten. The only thing I could focus on was the pleasure he was giving me. I felt it throughout my whole body.

"Kayleigh," Major said, getting my attention, "touch yourself for me."

With only a hint of a blush at the request, I rubbed my clit with him watching me. The look on his face was almost enough to make me come right then and there. The look was one of ownership and pure pleasure, it was totally hot.

"I'm close," I told him.

"I know." He grinned and replaced my fingers with his.

Just the feel of his fingers on me was enough to push me over the edge. I tried to keep my eyes on him, but the pleasure was just too much. I called out his name and grabbed at the sheets. I felt his rhythm change and managed to open my eyes. Seeing him come was never going to get old.

After he said my name about ten times, he collapsed on me. We were a sweaty mess, but I never wanted to move from that spot. Eventually Major rolled off me to dispose of the condom. He was back with me only moments later.

"I love you, Kayleigh," he whispered in my ear, as he pulled me close to him.

"I love you back," I told him. "Thank you for making this the best Valentine's Day a girl could ask for."

I heard the smile in his voice. "Just think, I have the rest of our lives to try and top it."

That made me laugh. "Happy Valentine's Day, Major."

"Happy Valentine's Day, Kayleigh."

Be My Valentine

The Promise Before

A Yellow River Pledge

Short Story

by

Lisa Colodny

Chapter 1

The asphalt under her feet was warm, sticky even as Jordan Chamberlain neared the parking spots furthest away from the Medical Examiner's office where her jeep was parked. Just as well, she thought, it would look out of place intermingled within the ocean of Mercedes and BMWs of the staff who worked there. True, the jeep was reliable, and the tires were new, but it was in desperate need of a paint job and the upholstery was stained from the previous owner. Jason had stressed over it for days once he'd brought the jeep home, scrubbing and cleaning on the seat's stains as if it were a disease. In the end, he'd given up; citing it would just have to do until they could afford something better. And that wouldn't come until their college loans were paid off.

They'd only been married a short while when he'd driven the vehicle home and parked it. The way he'd maneuvered it carefully alongside his own worn truck parked in the driveway of the small townhouse they shared brought a smile to her face every time she remembered it. She and Jason were born of the same cloth to loving, middle class parents, who worked hard to see they had everything they needed and most of what they wanted. Like her, he was grateful for the things in his life. Marrying him three years ago had been the happiest day of her life. They were like puzzle pieces, a perfect match, one with the other.

The car idling behind her, it's gears twitching and belching as if it were hungry, was a distraction. Discreetly, she slid her hand into her lab coat pocket, feeling thankful when her fingers wrapped around the cylinder of mace she kept close by. Although night fall was still a long away, the coroner's office wasn't exactly in a good area of town and the cover of darkness wasn't always required to conceal a crime. Her friend, Maria, never missed an opportunity to remind her the corpses didn't have to travel far to get to the morgue; most times the crime scene was nearby, sometimes within walking distance.

"I love to watch you walk!" The words spilled over his tongue slowly like a song, not a soft melodic one. His words were rough and staccato as he revved the car's engine in perfect harmony.

It probably would have been a better plan to continue walking the path towards her jeep, but the temptation was too much. Jordan found her head turn involuntarily in the direction of his voice.

"Jason?" her husband's name rushed from her lips, as if they were too hot to stay contained in her mouth. "What are you doing?' She made no attempt to conceal her anger at him or her relief in discovering there was no immediate danger.

"I've a surprise." He tapped the outside door of the truck for added affect. "Get in."

She stopped walking, coming to a halt at the vehicle's door to come face to face with him. "I only have an hour to pick up the trace evidence from the Palm Beach coroner's office." She resumed her pace, walking briskly as the distance between her and Jason's vehicle grew.

"There is no evidence. "He edged the truck closer to her before coming to an abrupt stop almost at her heels. "I asked Maria to help with a diversion."

"Diversion?" She turned back to him. "For what?"

"Valentine's Day is this weekend." He swallowed, as if the mere pleasure of the words to come couldn't be contained in his mouth. "I thought I'd surprise you."

"With?" She pulled the strap of her satchel higher on her shoulder and waited for him to respond.

"A Valentine's Day get away; now get in the car," his words were playful, yet impatient.

"Get away? I can't go away; I've so much work," she repeated, although her movement to the front of the car toward the passenger seat was a contraindication. "If I want to be offered a permanent position once my residency is completed, I need Dr Richmond's support." She turned to look back towards the coroner's office as if she'd lost something. "The Special Agent in Charge was here again yesterday." Excitement oozed from every pore of her body; it was as if she had a fever and needed medical attention. "I was able to observe the autopsy for the serial case."

She moved closer to him. "It was so exciting; I'd love to work with them more frequently on those types of cases," she paused. "Which is why I can't possibly go away, even for a day if I want to work here once my residency is completed."

"Maria spoke with Richmond. It's all been approved. You aren't due back in the lab until Monday." He watched as Jordan tossed her bag atop the back seat. "You've put in more hours per day than anyone else in the coroner's office since the day you walked through the door. It's been two years; your due the time away. And we're taking it."

Jordan fell obediently against the seat cushion and pulled the door closed almost in the same motion. Maria had been acting weird all morning, it should have been a clue that something out of the normal was going on. They'd been friends since college, even attended medical school together. Maria was an open book as far as Jordan was concerned. No one read could read her better. No doubt, Maria had offered to finish the cases assigned to Jordan so that she and Jason could have their time together. Just as well, Jordan mused. She didn't want Maria sulking through the Valentines weekend again like last year. Maria had the talent of picking the most emotionally unavailable women to become involved with. It was a mystery, how all her relationships seemed to fall apart only weeks prior to Valentine's Day.

Jordan makes a mental note to have Aimee, their other friend from college, check on Maria over the weekend during the weekend. Aimee and her husband, Mark, would no doubt enjoy a romantic dinner on Saturday but should be able to find a moment to meet Maria for a cup of coffee or slice of pizza to break up the hurt of being alone during the most romantic day of the year.

"Where are we going?" she finally asked once the car pulled away from the parking garage and headed south on the interstate.

"It's a surprise." He didn't look away from the road. "We'll be back on Sunday. Maria is driving your car back to our place; Aimee's picking her up and bringing her back here to her truck."

"You've worked out all the details." Her words were bitter, but she hadn't intended them to be so. Jason had spent a significant amount of time putting this together for her; it was a well needed break for them both. His schedule was similar in intensity to hers, starting his own consulting and construction business had been all consuming since graduation. Like everything he did, he gave the business his all. There were frequent weeks, when their only time together was the rustling of the blankets as one of them slid into bed.

"I have." He smiled across the seat to her. "And we are going to have an amazing weekend."

"Aren't we going home first so I can pack a bag?" Her mind was spinning, their townhouse was north of the coroner's office. The car was heading south, towards Miami.

"No." He smiled and nudged his head towards the back seat. "I packed a bag for you."

"Oh no," she whispered. Jason had no sense of what fabrics went with what. And he still wore the same tube socks he had worn in college. On Saturday mornings, he matched the color of the stripe on the socks to his athletic shorts. It was one of the things about him she both loved and hated, simultaneously. "You should have allotted time for me to pack for myself."

"I packed everything you'll need. Trust me." He patted her knee in a tender manner meant to comfort her and minimize her anxiety. "I wanted to surprise you. It would have spoiled it if you knew you'd be needing a suitcase."

The feeling of his hand against her knee was electric and felt the charge all the way to her core. They had both been so focused on their respective careers; it was as if time stood still and they were back in college and set to enjoy simply being together. True, they had only been married a few years, but there were moments it felt as if a lifetime had passed. She was suddenly grateful for the opportunity to be alone with him without a medical or construction distraction.

"Where are we going?" It was an innocent enough question, but the thoughts spinning about in her mind were anything but. The ache initiated by his hand on her knee burned like a wildfire. Wherever they were

154

headed, she hoped the destination was nearby. What she was really wondering was how long before she could feel him, all of him against her skin, twisting and turning her body into his until she was satiated, full and empty at the same time. It had been too long since they had made love for the shear enjoyment of it. Lately, it seemed more of a duty, a task to scratch off the list. Hopefully, once they arrived at their destination, they could lose themselves in one another. And they had three days to do it!

"South Beach?" she called out louder than she meant to and stifled a giggle as Jason attempted to conceal, he had been startled. "We're going to South Beach?"

"Nope," he sounded younger, juvenile almost. It was obvious by the rigidity of his shoulders, he was anxious to get their weekend started, too. "Just settle down and think about all the things you want me to do to you once we're alone." There was nothing juvenile about his words as she pictured his hands and lips exploring her body in a way only, he could. Jason had always been able to read her, know what her needs were even if she did not. Even many years ago as they fumbled through her first sexual experience, he had known what she wanted, what she needed to make the experience satisfying for them both.

"Promises, promises." She leaned against the window, hoping they were close and bothered less by what he had or had not packed for her.

Chapter 2

It was not until their car sped passed the city of Homestead and Jason merged onto State Road twenty-seven, she realized they were headed to the Florida Keys. The Keys, she twirled the destination around in her thoughts for several minutes. This was going to be an expensive weekend; no doubt, there would be no funds left in their discretionary account. Canned soup and McDonalds, that is what they would be dining on for the next month to pay off the weekend rendezvous.

"Key West?" she asked, with only a fraction of uncertainty. Unless, he had chartered a boat, the only other option was Cuba.

"Islamorada," he corrected her. "We couldn't afford Key West."

"Can we even afford this?" She waved her hand towards the windshield as if they arrived already.

"I just finished a job for a guy who owns a house down here. He offered me the beach house for three days in lieu of the labor charge for the project." Jason's smile was broad, his eyes squinting against the late afternoon sun as he went on. "The only things we have to pay for this weekend is food and drinks."

"Oh good," Jordan's thoughts were transient as the thought of Campbells soup and McDonald's for the next month all but dissipated leaving only a tinge of a bitter aftertaste. Her mind wandered involuntarily back to work. No doubt, Maria and Richmond were starting the last cases of the day. She knew Richmond well enough to know he'd only do to the corpse what had to be done. Whatever could wait for her return, would be waiting for her in the laboratory when she returned to work on Monday.

And Maria, would only process evidence that would not warrant a court assignment. She hated presenting evidence; if there was even a remote possibility the case would be presented in court. She'd finagle a way to pass it over to one of the other junior examiners, usually Jordan.

Testifying in criminal cases was a frequent requirement of the job, especially, if the FBI was involved. It seemed as if all their cases were similar to the one she'd just sat in on. It had been a complex case with a plethora of forensic evidence. Several young women, mostly prostitutes, had been raped and murdered. Their bodies dumped like trash along deserted or vacated buildings in Broward and Dade counties. Yet, even with all the forensic evidence, there were no suspects, no one in custody, and no unknown suspects, UNSUB as the FBI agents had termed them.

Her mind spun, neurons firing as if they were part of a July fourth celebration, at the thought of jumping on a jet plain with thirty minutes notice and flying across the country to work with local police on a serial crime. Someday, her heart raced, if she worked hard and did good work, the opportunity to work with the Violent Crimes division would present itself. Until it did, working with at the Coroner's office would have to suffice. And most days, it was enough; she loved her job. The only set back was the amount of time she was away from their home and Jason. Her mind was occupied again by the thought of working with the FBI; no doubt traveling all other the world would cut even deeper into her private life.

Jason's words behind the canvas of her thoughts were magnetic as she realized he was talking to her, waiting for a response. His impatient glances back and forth from the road in front of him to where she sat next to him was validation to them both that she had not heard a word he had said.

"I'm sorry." She dropped her hand apologetically on his leg. "What did you say?" There was no point in trying to pretend she had been listening; he would see right through the lie. They knew each other too well. "I was thinking about work."

"I asked if you ever regretted going into forensics." His words were soft, as his eyes darted back and forth form her to the road. "You and Aimee were both offered the same surgical residency and you were their number one match. If you had accepted, you would have had a regular nine to five job; our life together might be more stable with regular hours."

"I like the challenge of putting the pieces together and partnering with the police to bring criminals to justice." She smiled. "And your hours are only slightly better than mine."

"I know." His smile was contagious, boyish even as if he had crossed home plate after ushering the other base runners ahead of him. "But one day, neither of us will have to work this hard." He pulled her across the seat closer to the driver's seat. "And we will have a big house and new cars – "

"Those things are nice, Jason." She leaned against his shoulder. "But what's most important is that we have each other." She kissed his cheek. "That will always what I want most of all. I love you."

"Are you hungry?" he asked, as he cranked his neck towards the back seat. "These a small cooler with some fruit and cheese in the back. And some bottled water if you are thirsty.",

"No, but I would like to shower as soon as we get there." She looked down at her hands. "And I hope you packed my lotion from the nightstand. My hands are so dry, I had two waiting to be bathed this morning."

"Why doesn't Robert do that? He is after all, your assistant." Jason looked down to her hands momentarily. "Seems like that would be a task better suited for someone else, not a doctor. I mean, why doesn't Richmond assign a technician to bathe the bodies?"

Jason had never been an overtly arrogant man and she knew him well enough to better understand what he had meant by the question. She was not offended by his question and she did not think any less of him for the inquisition.

"Richmond is seldom involved in the day-to- day tasks of the business. He wanders in and out of everyone's office, self-absorbed in something that has little to do with the case." She smiled. "But he always seems to know everything about everyone. He's like a neighbor you discover has been spying on the others." She paused to collect her thoughts. "Robert will do anything that is asked of him. He's a thoughtful and hardworking assistant. And yes, he is more than capable of bathing the bodies in preparation for their autopsies." She pulled away just enough to leave a small distance between their legs. "He's cross trained in every forensic module available to the coroner's office. The task is one I've assigned to myself."

"Why would you do that? It's not like you don't have enough to do already."

"Because--" Her attention was focused on the road ahead. "It's the last human act that is afforded to them. Once the body has been bathed and any trace evidence collected, I can't really think of them as a person anymore."

She felt his surprise, knew he was taken aback by what she'd said. "Once they finish being bathed, they become evidence, a specimen to be dissected and studied." She exhaled. "Bathing them is the last human act and I'm grateful to be the one delivering it. If I think of them as anything else, I wouldn't be able to do this job for long."

"That's one of the many reasons I love you." He nodded his head in an overt attempt to conceal his watery eyes and changed the subject. "I don't think I packed your lotion, but we'll get some when we stop for gas. I love you, Jordan, more and more every day that we are together." He paused and took her hand. "And as long as I have you, I'll be the richest man in the world. I'd never ask for anything more."

Chapter 3

"Jordan?" Jason's words sounded far away, yet she knew was close by. The fragrance of his cologne was pungent, and she felt the warm air of his breath against her cheek. "Wake up, we're here."

"Already?" her words were disoriented as she straightened up and pushed as far back against the seat as she could and ran her hand through her hair, massaging it back into place.

"You napped the last little bit." Jason opened the truck door and pushed the seat forward enough to collect their bags from the back seat. He indicated to a small bag in the seat next to her. "I stopped a while back for gas and got you some lotion." He fought back a laugh. "It's not the same one that you have at home, but it must be pretty good. It was twelve dollars for that tiny bottle."

"Twelve dollars?" she repeated, as she opened the passenger door and climbed out into the afternoon sun. "I could have waited. We're only going to be here a few days, right." Its rays were warm against her face while the wind through her hair was cool and carried in it the fragrant odor of salt and something else. She inhaled deeper, fresh fish maybe?

The house was just as she imagined, set a few hundred yards from the raging rush of the water with a small white, wooden porch overlooking the surf as it washed over the sand. The palm trees were tall and skinny; some standing as straight as an arrow, while others were bent at odd angles, as if crippled by the weight of their long, green leaves. There were lounge chairs scattered about, most placed under the tiny shadows cast by the tree's palm leaves. Against the white sand of the beach, it looked more like dozens of charred campfires. Behind the line of palm trees, beyond the strip of the beach the water closest to the coast swirled aqua blue, its white caps crashing against the sand leaving a trail of shells and rocks that glistened like glass against the setting sun.

Jordan waited for Jason to make his way around the truck closer to her. "It's beautiful." The words slid from her lips as if she had not intended to share her thoughts. She turned back to the water and used her hand as a shield. "It's beautiful," she repeated, louder this time and with more conviction.

"Yes." He motioned her towards the house. "It is and it's all ours for the next few days."

Once they were inside, he dropped their bags at the door as if they were burning his hands and pulled her deeper into the space before latching the door behind him. The house was little more than a large room with a small kitchenette at one end and a bathroom that was surprisingly bigger than Jordan expected at the other. Even more surprising was the claw feet tub sitting caddy corner against the back wall just to the left of a grand window that overlooked the beach.

Outside, the fronds of the palm danced briskly with the wind and scratched lazily against the glass plane producing a rhythmic cadence. It was hypnotic; Jordan found herself wondering if the cushions of the sofa were as soft as she imagined. Did the linen carry the fragrance of the sea on the threads of its fabric? Or, was the scent of salt a figment of her imagination? Her eyes traveled the room impatiently; it took only a second to deduce there was no television, the door to the entertainment center simply covered an empty space. Just as well, neither of them would be watching much television anyway during their stay.

The largest piece of furniture in the room was the bed; it was so big, there was not room for a nightstand at either flank. Instead, the sides of the thick, mattresses kissed the sides of the walls at its edges. It was as if the walls were built around the bed instead of vice versa. It also meant both Jason and Jordan had to crawl from the foot of the bed to the head once both stepped out of their clothes and climbed in.

Chapter 4

"My God!" Jordan dropped her forehead against the pillow and whispered. "That was amazing." She breathed, pausing long enough to catch her breath before adding. "Both times."

Jason crawled along the long length of her body to rest his chin against the back of on her shoulder and pulled himself close enough to suckle a small patch of skin into his mouth. "Give me a minute and I'll be ready to go again.

"I think we need to take a break, maybe take a bath and grab a bite to eat." Her words were slurred as if she'd been drinking even though she hadn't had anything except water since they'd arrived at the beach house. She pulled the sheet tighter around her body, unbothered by the droplets of sweat that dropped from his chin and came to rest upon her shoulder blade.

"I think I'd like to take a swim first, then shower." He yanked the sheet away from them both as if it was burning his skin and jumped to his feet. "Can I have like fifteen minutes and I'll meet you in the shower?"

"Oh no." She wrapped the sheet around her damp body before pushing herself to her feet. "If we do that, one thing will lead to another and we'll never get dinner." She tied the sheet around her chest and drug the remainder behind her like a train on a wedding dress. "I skipped lunch again today; I'm hungry."

She flipped the shower on inside the small stall. "Besides, we don't need to christen the entire room on the first day." She stepped out of the sheet and folded it over the chair. "We need to pace ourselves. You go ahead and enjoy your swim."

"Think about where you want to go for dinner." He stepped into his swimming trunks and called to her distorted image in the shower. "I won't be long."

"Okay," she answered just as the sound of the water exploded against the shower floor. "It takes me longer to get ready than you. Even with the extra fifteen-minutes, you'll still be ready for dinner before me."

The warm water against her back and shoulders was pleasurable, almost to the extreme that she considered staying in the room and ordering take out from a nearby restaurant. It was a rarity to have this much free time with him. More often than not, their time together was cut short by work, hers more often than his. It was liberating to the extreme to consider both their offices were three hours away. Even if something urgent were to occur that required assistance, it would be a moot point by the time he or she could arrive on the scene.

It was as if they had turned back time and they were back at college without the responsibilities of his construction company or the coroner's office. It felt good to have Jason all to herself and to be the sole object of his concentration. Jordan turned the shower knob to the off position and stepped closer to the shower wall as the water dripped to a stop.

It took only a second to wrap up in a clean towel and pull the overnight bag he had packed for her atop the bed. Jeans, her mind catalogued as she sorted through the folded items. Two polo shirts, three bathing suits (all two pieces), two pairs of socks, and a single pair of sandals. Her toiletries, shampoo, conditioner, and brush were tucked in a small zipper case buried in the bottom of the bag.

To her dismay, she was without a bra (other than the one she was wearing) and there was not a nightgown or pajamas in sight. Apparently, Jason planned for her to sleep in the nude during their stay and did not expect she'd need a clean bra. And his choice of bathing suits left a lot to be desired. There were several one piece suits she'd preferred over the two-piece ones he'd packed. One of them she had not worn sent college; she wasn't even sure she could still fit into it.

These were the things about Jason that enamored her more and more every day of their life together. He could be child-like, adolescent almost, at times plotting and planning creative sexual excursions for them. Yet, possess the intellect and business savvy to build a successful construction company from the ground up and plan the most romantic interlude any adult man has ever considered. He was a man of many appetites and she was savoring the taste and texture of each engagement as if it were their last. That was one thing the Coroner's office had taught her early on, life was short, unexpected, and could be altered tragically at any minute.

Chapter 5

The restaurant was busy for a weeknight; it was tucked against the shore, no doubt the outside seating was in a perfect position to hear the crash of the surf as it smashed against the sand. As neither had a jacket or coat, Jason requested an inside table and pulled Jordan to the side to wait until they could be seated.

Jason's jeans were worn and faded; they were designer, expensive, and he had a tendency to wear them until they were ragged and practically hanging off his muscular form. His shirt, however, was like new, pressed and tucked into his jeans. He looked more like a graduate student, than a married, businessman. His dark hair could have used a trim; it was obvious he planned their trip quickly. Otherwise, he would have visited his barber and gotten decked out for their getaway.

The dark strands of hair around his chin and jawline were an indication he had not shaved earlier that morning. No doubt, his need to run by the construction site once before picking her up had thrown him off schedule. His thirty minute "pop in" had been nearly three hours. By the time he returned to their house to grab his bag and pack hers, he had less than an hour to get across 595 and up A1A to the Coroner's office. Intercepting Jordan before she made the drive to West

Palm for the fabricated evidence was a vital part of the scheme. Once she was en route, he would have no choice but to wait for her return. The entire plan would be in compromise.

"I'm sorry." He scratched at his chin and pointed with his fork to the vivid colors of the bikini top that was visible through the white shirt Jordan was wearing. "I was so focused on beachwear, I forgot about the essentials."

He leaned in closer to her, stretching his upper body as far across the small dining table as he comfortably could. "Of course, you could have just went without a bra." He looked around the room as if searching for someone. "You'd have fit right in."

"I wouldn't feel comfortable with that at all. I rinsed out the one I was wearing; its drying in the room." She checked her watch and motioned to Jason to top off her wine. "Is anyone watching the house?"

"Maria was going to stroll through tomorrow and make sure everything is okay." He laughed. "It's not like there's much in the house that anyone would want to steal. There are much better homes in our neighborhood that would make a better target for thieves."

"After the washer hose burst last year and flooded the entire first floor, I'm a little weary of leaving for very long." Jordan sipped at the wine.

"That's why she's just walking through to make nothing has overheated or is leaking." Jason advised, as he sliced several portions of steak and forked tiny pieces into his mouth. "I wanted her to stop by on Saturday, but she said she had made a date at the last minute." He shook his head. "I don't understand why she feels she has to sneak around. She shouldn't feel she has to hide the that she's gay."

"It's her father." Jordan explained. "Her father runs in conservative circles; he is a powerful man in Dade county." Jordan assessed the tables nearby to ensure her conversation was private. "Her relationship with him has never been good; he'd never forgive her the embarrassment and humiliation it would cause him." She swallowed. "I am glad she's not spending Valentine's Day alone."

She pushed the dinner plate towards the center of the table and eyed the dessert cart as the server passed by. "For the longest time, other than the women she dated, only Aimee and I knew." She waved to the server and pointed to a thin slice of key lime pie. "Why didn't you ask Aimee to check on the house? She lives closer to us and would not be working on Saturdays. Marc's dental practice isn't open on weekends; they should both be home."

"Aimee didn't return my call, I figured they must be busy," He looked away. "And I knew Maria would help me out. She always does."

"Yes, she does." Jordan's thoughts turned to college and a psychology class Maria had helped Jason pass. Jason's analytical mind had struggled from day one in the class. Even though, she, Maria and Aimee had all been in the class together. It had been Maria who had come to his aid. Jordan smiled, the memory igniting a hum in her heart. It had been many years since she had thought about that period in their lives. It seemed far away most days. Yet, there were other instances when the memory was closer as if it were yesterday and they were younger, much younger with dreams yet realized and scars yet to be delivered.

She and Jason had an innocence back them, vulnerability unmarred by autopsy or a million-dollar business loan. Jason had taken a big risk going out on his own before establishing a solid base of clients and accounts, He had not doubted himself, never considered his business would not be successful. On the other hand, she worried all the time that she might not be good enough at putting the pieces together to aid the police in their investigations or work with the FBI. She hoped her skill and motivation, along with her work ethic would guarantee her a position with the Coroner's office once she completed her residency in a few months, but there was always a chance they'd choose someone else, someone better, smarter.

She leaned in closer to him and took his hand. "Do you ever imagine what our life will be like in five years, ten years?" There was a brief pause before she went on. "Will we still be 'us' or more closely resemble one of those couples we point and laugh at?"

He took her hands and pulled her as close to him as he could. "Jor, we are who we are and that won't change. Hopefully, we'll be living in a big house on the water instead of the crappy little town house we live in now." He paused only long enough to catch his breath as the words flowed from his lips like honey. "We'll both be driving expensive cars that we'll trade in every year even though there's nothing wrong with the car." His eyes darted back and forth as if her were reading the words from a cue card. "I will learn how to golf just for the hell of it. And you can play tennis with the Los Olas moms."

"Aren't those the couples we make fun of?" There was laughter as she finished the sentence but also truth in the cadence of her words. "And what about children?" She swallowed not bothered by the sound that escaped from her throat as the saliva slid past her esophagus.

"The hours your job requires even now is substantial," he whispered. "Can you imagine how it will be once you're assigned cases all on your own?" He dropped her hands. "Let's just focus on our weekend together. We've plenty of time to talk about children and when is the best time to start planning a family." He kissed her hand. "We both are in agreement that we can't start one any time soon, right?"

She nodded. After all he was right. Even if they both agreed they wanted to start a family immediately, they could not afford it. It would be several years before they could have a new house with enough room for a nursery and a yard, possibly a nanny to help with the baby once Jordan returned to work post maternity leave. It was there, tied up in a nice little box with a bow. One day, they would open the box and live the life she dreamed of.

Chapter 6

The setting sun as it kissed the horizon and disappeared seemed to be little more than an alarm. It was as if the sun's rays clapped and clang against one another and echoed across the beach giving notice to beachgoers that it was time to leave. And one by one, they did until Jordan and Jason found themselves, practically alone on the thin blanket placed just outside their back porch.

The wine bottle between them was empty but remnants of the dark liquid remained in the paper cups staggered within the sand piles. Paper plates partially filled with crackers, cheese and grapes were at either end of the beach blanket, while two haphazardly folded beach towels were propped a small Styrofoam cooler.

"You look amazing in that suit." Jason pulled her atop his body, positioning her hips like fine china between the cradle of his legs. He slid his fingers under the strap of her top and pulled at the snaps until the thin strand of material separated and fell her under her arms.

"I would have preferred the blue one piece." She answered, lifting her arms around his neck and finding his lips with her own.

"If I packed that one," he said, as he untied the strap around her neck. "I wouldn't have been able to do that." He gathered the suit top in his hand and pulled it away dropping it in the sand beside them.

She pressed herself as tightly against his body as she could, enjoying the way his chest hair felt against her breasts and the hardness of his erection between her legs. She felt him push his swimming trunks down just enough to free his penis.

"Jason," she whispered, one hand wrapped around his penis while the other pushed his lips against her breast in contradiction. "We can't do this here. Someone might see." The familiar tightness between her legs was overwhelming and she opened herself wider to accommodate the length of him at her core.

"It's isolated here, no one's inside the other house. And-" he paused long enough to slide the bottom of her suit down her legs. "It will be dark soon. No one's watching us." He sat up with her in his lap and flipped them both, so that her back was on the blanket. Wasting no time, he suckled his way down her body, licking her breasts, tonguing her nipples, trailing a path along her abdomen, and locking lips with the tiny nerves between her legs. Jason pulled her thighs atop his shoulders; his mouth never breaking contact with her core and took her breasts in his hands.

Jordan danced against him, moving her groin against his mouth as quickly as she could to prolong her pleasure. It was like being on a runaway train, its abrupt turns and bumps against the tracks was almost painful and she pulled him away by the hair to provide a moment of relief. She was sorry as soon as he broke contact, and the pressure began to dissipate. It was too soon, she needed more, and she pushed him back to his task between her legs.

Seconds later, she was falling, falling around him, pulsating with the pleasure provoked by his mouth. He was like the air to her breath, the light in the darkness, and water to the fire. And she held onto him as if her life depended on it. It was a full minute before she felt him moving, kissing his way back up her body and sliding his penis into her in a single motion.

Jordan had always been intrigued by the emotions that played on Jason's face as they made love. He was an intense lover; he always had been even the first few times when sex was new to her. His attention to the details of love making had never disappointed her. Even after the honeymoon was over, it was his personal goal to see to that she was satisfied, regardless of how tired either of them were. If they were going to make love, he wanted to get it right each and every time.

She continued to study his face as his steadied himself above her, his hands planted firmly on the sand at either side of her head and slapped his body against her. He was close to his release; she could tell by the way he squinted his eyes together and bit at his bottom lip just as reached orgasm and emptied himself into her.

"Oh no." He fell against her, his body only partially on the blanket, his breath coming in great gasps. He kissed her shoulder and fingered her breast with the tip of his finger until it peaked hard against his skin.

"What is it?" She turned her body to his as if he were a full-length pillow.

"I didn't pack your pills this afternoon when I grabbed your things." He pulled her into his arms and bit at the skin of her neck.

"Pills?" she repeated, although she knew he was referring to her birth control pills. Would it be so bad she thought? To be pregnant, to be starting the family she dreamed of? Did they really need to wait until they had more money, more material things? Deep down, she really didn't think so. When it happened, they'd be ready. And if they weren't ready, they'd work to get themselves ready.

"A few nights won't make a difference will it?" he asked, as he sat up and pulled his swimming trunks back on.

"It can make a difference, yes," she answered, as she slid into her suit bottoms. "There are reports of women getting pregnant from a single missed dose." Jordan tied the top around her neck and held the material over her breasts and motioned for him to reconnect the top.

"We'll just have to improvise from this point on and be careful." He offered his hand to help her up from the blanket and draped the sandy blanket over his arm. "We need to put that tub to use."

"I agree." She smiled, before following him into the beach house.

Chapter 7

"We need a tub like this," Jordan words were like a song as she squeezed the bathwater from a sponge onto her breasts and leaned against his chest as if he were a bed pillow.

"We shower together." His words were defensive, but Jordan knew he had not meant for them to be.

"It's not the same." Her words were sleepy, as her hand found his penis and she coaxed it to attention. "We have sex in the shower on our way to our respective jobs." She turned around in the water to face him. "We're in a hurry and sometimes it feels like we're checking it off our to do list."

"I love you, Jordan." Anxiously, he pushed her back against the tub's edge and fell atop her in a single motion. "Since the day we met, I've never wanted anyone but you." He pushed her legs apart with his hand and filled the empty space with his growing erection. "The empire I'm building, I'm building for you. One day, you won't want for anything."

"I love you, too," she said against his lips, grimacing as he pushed himself into her. "As nice as all those things sound, they won't make us happy. Not really."

"No." His smile was boyish, as gripped the ends of the tub for support and slammed against her. "I didn't mean that; I just meant it would be nice to have those things AND each other."

She could tell by the sound he was making that he was nearing his climax; she wasn't surprised when he pulled his engorged member from her body, jumped to his feet, and emptied himself into a wash rag that was hanging over the tub.

He tossed the soiled rag into the corner and fell back against the other side of the tub; his hand disappearing under the water. "I can't believe I forgot the dammed pills."

She felt his hand against her thigh as he minimized the distance to rest between her legs.

"I'm tired." She placed her hand against his. "Let's call it a night?"

"You sure?" He rubbed her center, impatiently. "I can be quick."

"I'm sure," She kissed his other hand. "Let's save some of that energy. It's only the first night." She stepped from the tub and wrapped herself up in a thick, furry, bath towel. "Did I see chocolate covered strawberries in the cooler?"

He stepped into the space behind her and wrapped his arms around her. "You did and another bottle of wine is chilling."

"Not sure about more wine." She stopped near the bed and collected her bag. "I'm not sure if it was intentional or not but you didn't pack any pajamas for me, either." She stepped into her underwear. "Give me one of your cotton shirts?"

He rummaged through his bag. "We could just sleep in the nude?" He held a shirt out to her. "I can if you will?" His smile grew wide as he went on. "Remember when we first got married, we tried that?"

"Yeah, for like three days," she laughed. "It just wasn't very comfortable." She held out her hand to him. "Give me the shirt." She pulled it over her head and moved quickly to towards the bed. "Are we having the strawberries in the bed?"

"We can." He stepped into his underwear. "Give me a second to get them on a plate. You sure you don't want some more wine?"

"Just a little to go with the strawberries." She propped herself against the headboard and waited for him to return with their snack. What was that saying about the life not being measured by the number of breaths taken? She smiled, warmed by the thought of all the moments he had taken her breath away and inspired to know he would no doubt take many more as they grew older together. She was a lucky woman in more ways than one.

Chapter 8

It was not the sun peeking through the curtain that woke her up; it was a combination of the closing of the door and the sounds Jason made as he crept closer to the bed with a breakfast tray of food in his arms.

"Where'd you get all that?" she asked in reference to the stack of pancakes she could easily make out from the bed. Once he drew nearer, she could see he had a plate of eggs and bacon as well as a dessert plate of assorted muffins and croissants.

"There's a diner across the street." He placed the tray on the nearest table and handed her a cup filled with streaming coffee. He pointed to the tray. "What's your preference?"

"A little of it all." It was like being a child in a candy store. "Can you slice a small portion of the pancakes, few pieces of bacon with some scrambled eggs." She studied the plate of pastries. "And that chocolate croissant on top." She watched as he performed as instructed and turned back to face her with the plate poised out as if it were an award she had won.

"What is the plan for today?" she asked around the bite of syrup coated pancakes in her mouth.

"I thought we'd drive home after lunch?" His words were succinct as if he were testing the water before venturing into the deep end of the pool.

"I thought we were staying till tomorrow?"

"That was before I realized I didn't pack your birth control pills. Three days without taking them might be pushing it a bit."

"Would it be so bad?" The words jumped from her mouth of their own volition. Judging by the look on his face, she wished she could force them back in her mouth and pretend she had not asked the question.

"Jordan?" He slid into the place next to her. "I thought you we agreed that we'd wait?"

"You agreed," she clarified. "I just didn't disagree. I know that I do want children someday and I'm not sure you do."

"Did I ever say that I didn't?" He was impatient bordering on angry. "Just because I didn't say I do doesn't mean I don't. I just want to wait until we can afford to have them."

"Five years?" Jordan asked. "Three? Ten?"

"I don't know baby." He kissed her cheek. "We will know when the time is right. You'll see." He pulled a single rose from under the blanket. "It's Valentine's day, let's just focus on the present for now. The future will take care of itself."

"Where you get that?" She smiled and took it from his hand.

"Same place I got breakfast." There was a pause before he handed her a small jewelry box. "This I brought with me."

"What's this?"

"Open it and see." He stuffed several bites of pancakes into his mouth and watched as she opened the box.

It was hard to conceal her surprise; the ring was beautiful. The middle stone was a sapphire, so blue it appeared almost black surrounded by tiny diamonds. Other than her engagement and wedding rings, she had never seen a piece of jewelry more perfect. "Jason," she took it from the box. "How can we afford this? This trip – "

He cut her off. "The trip was pretty much a wash; asl I said is we have to pay for our food. I brought the wine with us, so we've expensed very little so far." His eyes were soft, sad almost as he went on. "I know you, Jordan. You haven't asked for much; you always seem to make do with whatever we have. You didn't get a honeymoon, not a real one I mean. We couldn't afford it."

"I have what I need, Jason. And if the house we have is the only one we ever have; it will be enough because it's ours. Fancy cars and trips are nice but that's not what's important in life. And it's certainly not who I am. I hope you know that."

"I do." He kissed her hand. "And it only makes the desire to give you those things greater. You are the love of my life and I'm going to spend the rest of our life together reminding you of that."

"Promises, promises," she said, pulling him closer towards her and praying that he would be true to his word.

The Surprise Within

A Cliffhaven Coven Series

Short Story

by

Mary Dean

Chapter 1

Alex

It's almost Valentine's Day. Candy hearts are sold in small boxes. Chocolate everything is available in heart shapes. Valentines are given to secret and known crushes. Couples bend over backwards to prove their love to each other. Greeting cards have their moment to shine.

I can't stand it.

I am not against love. I am a big fan of it. I love my husband Nix to the moon and back. He is my rock, my protector, my best friend. But I don't need a cheesy saying on card stock and a box of candies that taste like chalk to prove it. He already does that with loving me. The man almost died to save me! I think he's shown it enough. But that brings me to the dilemma I'm in.

Nix loves Valentine's Day. Yes, you heard that right. You'd expect him to be annoyed by it and annoyed to do anything, right? Well, you'd be wrong. He loves all the cheesy romantic things. And the cheesier the better in his mind. I know he already made us reservations at our favorite Italian restaurant, Franscesca's in our small beach town of Cliffhaven. And I am sure he has some sweet gesture planned.

Nix doesn't know about my distaste for this holiday. He doesn't know that while I find the cheesy sayings funny, they also make me want to puke a little. I just haven't had the heart to break his spirits. Part of my anti-Valentine's Day feelings might have something to do with being a teenager on the run from an evil magic being with my mother and never getting to do the fun give-your-crush-a-valentine thing. My Valentine's Days were a cheap box of chocolate from my mom and us watching some cheesy romantic comedy that was on television. It wasn't until a few years ago that Nix and I were reunited and became the couple we always wanted to be.

I remember our first Valentine's Day. I came home from the store to find the house lit by candles and rose petals leading to our bedroom. When I reached the bedroom, there was Nix on the bed, naked, waiting for me. How can a girl say no to that?

Then the following year he surprised me with a trip to Niagara Falls and it was one of the most romantic experiences of my life. I just went along with it all. I didn't want to let him know that he put a lot of heart and work into making a holiday I didn't really like so special. I told myself after last year I would tell him before the next Valentine's Day arrived. Well it'll be here in a few days and I haven't had the courage to say anything. And now I think it'll be too late. I am sure he already has plans in the works. But those plans might be ruined. Not because I am going to be honest with him about how I feel. But because I might be sick with the flu.

I have been throwing up a lot lately and feeling really under the weather. Thankfully, I own my own small accounting business and I work from home. Clients didn't know I had to rush to the bathroom to throw up sometimes while updating their financial spreadsheets. I have been hiding it from Nix, too. It's only been a couple days. I just know he will worry and I don't want him to. So I am just riding out this flu until I feel better.

****

Nix

I hear Alex get up again in the middle of the night. She is trying to be quiet, but I hear what she's really doing in the bathroom. She's throwing up. And that has me concerned. The first night I thought it was just the junk food we ate. But it's been a couple nights since and she gets up at least once to throw up. I wonder if it's during the day while I am at work, too. I usually don't want to make her feel uncomfortable that I can hear her throwing up so when she comes back into the room, a fresh mint smell on her lips, I pretend to be asleep. But not tonight. I sit up and turn on the light and wait for her to emerge from the bathroom.

"Oh, hey," she says, as she walks back into the bedroom. She is shocked to see me looking at her. "What are you doing up?"

"Waiting for you," I say, as I pull back the covers for her and she slides into bed next to me. The mint smell hits my nose. She snuggles into her spot and pulls the blanket over herself.

"I just had to go to the bathroom. Too much water before bed," she tries to explain. "Goodnight." She shuts her eyes as if she is going to go right back to sleep.

I don't follow her lead. "We need to talk," I tell her.

She opens her eyes and then sits up. "Is this where you break up with me?" she teases.

I chuckle. "Not a chance." I pull her into my arms. That's my favorite feeling, My arms protectively wrapped around her. There was a time when I thought I'd never have this, so I don't take it for granted. That's why I can't just go along with acting like nothing is going on. "I know you were throwing up. And you have been for the past couple nights."

"Oh," is all she says.

"What's going on Alex?" I move to look into her eyes.

"I've just been sick lately. Maybe I'm catching a flu." She shrugs.

"I'd feel better if you got yourself checked out." I try to stop the panic at the thought that she is really sick from taking over.

"I'm fine. It'll pass." She pats my chest as if to reassure me.

"I'd still feel better if you saw Dr. Rosenbaum," I insist.

"I really don't think it's anything. I just have a stomach bug. It'll be gone in a few days."

I look at her with concern. "Can you just humor me and do it? It might be a waste of time. But I'd feel better if you saw the doctor."

"Okay," she says hesitantly. She cuddles back down into the sheet. "Now can we please go to sleep?"

I kiss her forehead. "Goodnight." I turn off the lamp and lay on my side, still worried that something more is going on.

"Don't you have your own house to drink lemonade at?" My sister, Rachel, asks the next day, as she comes into the kitchen at our mom's house, where she also lives with her two year old daughter Abby.

"You know nothing beats Mom's homemade lemonade." I take a sip and smile.

"True." Rachel looks out the window. I chuckle. I know whose truck she is looking for. Zeke's. He's our mom's friend's son. She recently passed away and our mom took him in until he can get a place of his own. He's a cool dude actually. I even gave him a job at my construction company. But my sister and him don't get along. Something about mud and dolls as kids.

"He's not here," I tell her.

"Who?" She quickly looks at me. "I wasn't looking for anyone," she says defensively.

"Sure you weren't." I smirk, as I bring my glass of lemonade up to my lips for the final sip. "You can't fool me, Rach. I am very observant."

She glares at me and then says, "oh yeah?" She gives me that look she has when she's up to no good. "Tell me, what are you doing for Valentine's Day?"

I frown confused. What did that have to do with anything? Then it hits me. "Nice try. You aren't getting any info so you can tell Alex. She will just have to wait for the surprise." I laugh. My wife was not the most patient person. Growing up she always peeked at her presents before Christmas. Because I was her best friend I was sworn to secrecy but a smart part of me was worried for her because what if Santa found out? The memory also makes me chuckle. It was simpler times but I wouldn't trade today for anything. I don't have to pretend I only have friendship feelings for her.

"You know she hates Valentine's Day, right?" Rachel blurts out, almost excitedly.

"What are you talking about?"

"Alex. She hates Valentine's Day," Rachel repeats slower, as if I am too stupid to understand.

"You don't know what you are talking about." I stand up and take my glass to the sink. If I left my dirty glass out my mother would not be happy with me. Her house is open to me whenever, but I can't be a slob.

"For being so observant, you really aren't. Alex can't stand Valentine's Day. She thinks it's lame." Rachel takes a seat at the kitchen table and looks at me smugly.

"No way. She loves Valentine's Day," I defend, and then ponder. It is always me doing the grand gestures. She does wear a new piece of lingerie that I always can't wait to take off of her. But other than that, nothing. It never bothered me. I figured Valentine's Days surprises were the husband's job. But now I am questioning if there is more to it.

"She loves what you do for her. But she can't stand the holiday. Every year she complains how cheesy it is and she can't wait for it to be over," Rachel reveals. She must read the look on my face. "Sorry, Bro." Her voice doesn't sound like she's sorry at all.

"Dammit," I throw down the towel I just used to dry my glass. "I had big plans this year. I was going to take her out to dinner to Francesco's and pay to have her serenaded. Then I was going to decorate the house in balloons and roses. I even picked out balloons with cheesy but cute sayings." I ran my hand through my hair wondering if I had time to stop the floral and balloon order.

"Yeah." Rachel laughs. "Sounds like a nightmare for her. You know she hates attention on her."

"Why do you know about her hate for Valentine's Day and I don't?" I question her, hoping to find some sliver of proof she is lying.

"Because she's not my wife. We are like sisters and sisters talk. Plus, she doesn't want to hurt your feelings."

"What do I do now?" I ask, feeling disappointed. She shrugs, looking satisfied. I shake my head. Of course, my wife would be different and not want anything done on Valentine's Day. I guess it's another thing that made her so unique. I sigh. "Well I need to go and handle some stuff."

"Good luck," I hear Rachel say to me, with humor in her tone, as I walk out the door.

Chapter 2

Alex

"Hi, Alex," Dr. Rosenbaum says to me, as she enters the examination room. She's in her 60's and has known me since I was a kid. She actually helped deliver me. Sometimes it's still awkward seeing people that knew me growing up because they also knew me as the girl who disappeared with her mom, was presumed dead, and then showed back up one day. As she enters the room, she is nothing but smiles and that eases some of my worry. They had me take a urine and blood test. That concerned me. What did they think was wrong with me?

"Hi Dr. Rosenbaum. Is everything ok?" I am not even trying to hide my nervousness.

"Oh yes, Sweetheart." She pulls up a chair next to the exam bench I'm sitting on. She pulls open the folder she is holding and hands me the results. I read them over quickly and then I reread them to make sure I read them right. I look at her. She nods with a smile.

"How can this be?" I am still not believing the words I am seeing.

"Well I think it's a little too late to explain to you how it works," she laughs slightly, and normally so would I if I wasn't so freaked out.

I'm pregnant.

The thought didn't even occur to me. Okay, that's a lie. I sort of wondered about it, but I was on birth control. I have been taking it regularly. Then I remembered a few months ago I had gotten the days mixed up, but I had done that before and been fine.

"How far along am I?" I quickly ask.

"About five weeks," she tells me. And that matches when I screwed up my pill days. "We could do an ultrasound today."

Part of me wants to tell her yes. But I can't have this moment without Nix. "I'd like to make an appointment another day for that if that's okay." She nods and she sees me out of the room. I tell the receptionist I'll call in a day or so to make my next appointment. The whole drive home I can't get my head around the fact that Nix and I are going to be parents. I wasn't ever sure if I wanted this. But spending time being an aunt to Abby the last few years has really hit my heart, and I do want that with Nix. I am just not sure if it's what he wants. We always agreed to wait to even talk about having kids.

"I'm home," I announce, as I walk through the front doorway. Nix is on the couch watching some movie with a lot of loud explosions. He looks up and gives me a faint smile. He seems off. I figure it's just him being worried about me.

"What did Dr. Rosenbaum say?" He shuts off the television, gets up off the couch, and walks over to me as I set my purse down on the kitchen table. Then I pick it up again. The results are in there and I'm not ready to tell him. He looks at me worried.

"Everything is good. Just something in my stomach. It'll pass soon," I tell him not actually lying. There is something in my stomach, a baby. He or she will pass soon, when I give birth.

"Thank you for going." He hugs me and I hug him back lightly. Now that I know there is a being inside me it I feel like even the smallest hug will make it known. I know I am not really showing. But if my pregnancy is anything like Rachel's I will start showing in a month or so. I feel like magic beings show more in their pregnancy. Abigail, Nix and Rachel's mom, says it's because of the magic forming.

"I'm going to go lay down." I push back from his embrace.

"Good idea. Rest is the best thing for you. Let me know if you need anything. I love you." He leans forward and kisses my forehead.

"I love you too," I reply and then head down the hall to our bedroom. I'm not tired. I have too much on my mind. I close the door behind me. I eye the bathroom and I decide to take a bath. That always relaxes me. I turn on the water and undress. As I wait for the tub to fill, I look at myself in the large mirror above the long sink. I look at my stomach. It looks like it normally does, flat and toned. But it also looks different to me. I run my hands over it. There is a child forming in there, a magic being that is half me and half Nix. The thought makes me smile.

"Everything okay?" I hear Nix's voice in the bedroom. The bathroom door is open and I can see him looking at me. There is concern in his eyes. But there is also hunger looking at me naked. Nix and I are still in the honeymoon stage. We can't get enough of each other most days. I don't think we will ever be out of it. I still get butterflies before I see him and just hearing his voice brings excitement to my entire being. "Is your stomach upset?" He looks at my hands that are on my stomach. I quickly move them away.

"No, I'm fine." I shake my head. I'm not lying. I don't feel sick at that moment. I then turn my body towards him. "Do I look, uh, different?" This is my way of seeing if he notices a change. I should just tell him, but I can't seem to find the words. I don't know why. Maybe it's the uncertainty. I don't want to find out how he feels when I am not sure myself.

"You look beautiful as always." He walks towards me. "Wait, no, you do look different."

My eyes widen. He can tell. He knows. I brace myself for the truth of his feelings. He reaches me and I feel him take me in his arms. His breath is hot on my neck. "You look even sexier today. It's like you are glowing."

"What?" I can't hide the panic in my voice. I look at my hands. They look the same.

Nix chuckles. "Relax. I just meant there is a certain glow to you right now. You look even more radiant." He leans down and gives me a sweet kiss. I look up. I see the concern in his eyes. He now looks as if he's trying to read my expression. "Are you sure Dr. Rosenbaum said everything was okay?"

I nod. I look behind me at the tub that is almost filled to the top. I remove myself from Nix's grasp and rush to the tub and turn the water off. I feel the cold porcelain hit my leg and that reminds me that I am naked. I don't feel embarrassed, though. I never am when I am with Nix. I stand up and then lift my leg and dip a toe into the water. The temperature is perfect.

"Mind if I join you?" Nix asks, already pulling off his shirt. I don't speak for a moment. No matter how many times I see him with his shirt off, his strong body always distracts me. I'll be honest, I have even drooled before. I sometimes can't believe that he is mine. "I take that as a yes." He smirks and that's when I realize I never said anything. I just stood there staring at him. He pulls down his sweats and I can't help but smile at what he reveals. I don't stand and stare this time. I get into the tub, leaving room for him to sit behind me like he prefers. We love taking baths together. As a wedding gift, Nix redid the tub so that it would fit us both comfortably. I feel him getting into the water behind me. I lean my back against him and his hand ends up on my stomach. I feel a small shock. I stiffen. Did he feel that? If he did, he isn't reacting.

"How do you feel about kids?" I blurt out the question without even thinking.

"What?" I can hear the surprise in his voice.

"Nothing." I shake my head.

"No, no." He turns my shoulder so I am half facing him. "You just caught me off guard. Kids? They are okay, I guess. Abby's my favorite of course," he laughs at his own joke.

I laugh, too, then shake my head. "No, I mean about us having kids." I look at him with fear in my eyes at his answer. I hope he doesn't tell me he isn't interested in being a dad. Before today's visit I would have been okay with that answer. We would be happy with being the coolest uncle and aunt ever. But being just an uncle and aunt duo is out of the question now. We are going to be parents.

"Sure, down the line. But there is no rush." He pulls me to him and kisses my neck. I decide to drop it and get lost in his affection. It's my favorite distraction.

****

Nix

I watch Alex sleep. She is in a deep sleep. I guess I wore her out. My ego is boosted. Don't get me wrong, I'm tired. She knows how to make me feel things no other woman ever has. And I've been with plenty of women. I'm no self-proclaimed gigolo, but I had my time where I slept with whoever only caring about my pleasure. But Alex changed that. She tamed me. And I couldn't be happier. But she was off tonight. Not sexually. That was great as always. What was off was how she was acting before. When she came home from the doctor's, she seemed to have a heavy mind. She stated that it was a good report and nothing was wrong. I didn't sense that she was lying. But I did sense she wasn't telling me everything. Then I saw her in the bathroom looking at her body in the mirror. Did she gain weight? Did the doctor say anything about her body? To me she was perfect.

Then the kids question came out of nowhere. We hadn't really talked about kids much. We had agreed we wanted to focus on just being married for a while. Was she wanting kids now? Did I want kids yet? I honestly didn't know. It wasn't until the last few years that I even thought it would be a possibility. That's only because I know Alex will be an amazing mother. But there is no rush.

I look over at Alex sleeping and decide I need to do the same. I have work in the morning. I gave the crew Valentine's Day off so there's just one more day of work before break. Thinking of Valentine's Day bums me out a little bit. I was able to cancel everything and get most of my money back. I feel like something is missing. And it's my Valentine's Day celebration. But what's the point if she isn't into it.

Chapter 3

Nix

"Ready for tomorrow Romeo?" Rachel says to me, when I walk into the trailer that is the office on the job site. She is typing away on the computer. We are working on building a large house. It's a good paying project, but it's also stressful. This client is picky and they have changed their minds a few times on some things. But that's part of the job.

"Ready for the day off? Sure am," I respond. I know what she's getting at, but I'm playing dumb.

"I mean whatever grand thing you are doing for Alex."

"I'm not," I inform her. I hear the typing stop and look up at her. She looks shocked. "What?" I ask.

"You aren't doing anything for Alex tomorrow?" She looks at me as if I am crazy.

"No. I listened to what you said. She's not into it."

"Don't listen to me! What do I know? I fell for a man who was just using me and ended up single and pregnant. I am not one to give relationship advice."

I look at her confused. "You said she doesn't like Valentine's Day. So, what is the point in going all out if she doesn't like it?" I am shocked she isn't agreeing with me.

"I just said she doesn't like Valentine's Day, not that she doesn't love what you do. Every girl wants to be spoiled. And besides, I was just being a brat."

"That's not new," I joke. A wadded-up piece of paper goes past my head. That just cracks me up more.

Seriously, Nix, don't listen to me. If you want to spoil your wife on Valentine's Day, don't let me stop you."

I shrug. "It's too late. I already canceled everything."

"Me and my big mouth," I hear her mutter.

Now I am conflicted again. Does Alex want me to do something? I guess I'll find out tomorrow night.

****

Alex

After I finish my work for the day, I decide to watch a Hallmark movie. Nix won't be home for a few hours. These movies are cheesy, predictable, and my favorite. The one I watch is about a man who hates Valentine's Day but the woman he is in love with loves Valentine's Day. He is always against doing anything. But he decides to surprise her and plans a romantic Valentine's Day evening and proposes to her at the end. My hopeless romantic heart is filled. Then an idea comes to me. That's how I'll tell Nix about the baby. Our baby. I'll plan some romantic gesture. That will be perfect. I just have to figure out what he's doing already. I decide to call someone I am sure can give me a hint if not spill all the plans Nix has.

"Hey Alex," Rachel says, as she answers her phone.

"Hey Rachel. How are you?" I ask and I genuinely am asking how she is. She has had a rough couple years. She went from a teenager who was wrapped up in her friends and her boyfriend to a single mother learning how to be independent. She of course has her mom and us to lean on, but it's not the plan I'm sure she had for herself. I admire Rachel. She is so strong. She also seems to know everyone's business all the time so I am sure she knows what Nix is planning.

"I'm good. Just working." I can hear her typing in the background.

"Is your brother around?" I ask, hoping he is out on the job site and not doing paperwork.

"He's meeting with the customer. Did you need him?" she asks, concerned.

"No. I was actually hoping he wasn't near you," I admit.

"Ooooh." I hear her stop typing. "What's up?" She sounds very intrigued. I have to laugh. Rachel loves gossip.

"I was wondering if you could give me any hints on what Nix has planned for us for Valentine's Day." After I say it, I realize how weird it sounds asking my husband's sister what romantic plans he has in store for us.

"Oh," she says and then is silent. That is not like Rachel. She usually would tease me for trying to get information or spill it right away. But as soon as I asked my question, her tone changed from intrigued to something else.

"What?" I ask after a minute of silence.

"He sort of took some stupid advice from someone and changed his plans," she says hesitantly.

"What sort of advice? From who? What plans changed? You have to give me more Rachel."

"Well." She lingers and then sighs. "He was over the other day and he was acting like he knows everything." I can just see her rolling her eyes. "So, to prove he was wrong I sort of told him you hate Valentine's Day."

"What?!" I can't believe what I'm hearing. That probably crushed him. There was a reason I couldn't break it to him how I really felt. "What did he say?"

"Well, he argued at first and then it seemed to make sense to him." She was talking fast like a child who was in trouble trying to explain their side. "Today when I asked him what his plans were, he told me he canceled everything. I'm so sorry Alex!"

"I can't believe this," I say, not meaning to make her feel bad.

"I told him not to listen to me. But he said it was too late and there was no point if you didn't like it."

"It's not that I don't like what he does. It's that it's not my thing. But I appreciate what he does," I explain to her as if it'll matter.

205

"I tried to explain that, but I think my big mouth ruined it as usual. I'm sorry Alex." I can hear the regret in her voice. I'm not mad at her. She was just going off what I always complain to her. I just never thought she would tell Nix and it would cause him to cancel his Valentine's Day plans.

"It's fine. Don't worry about it," I assure her. "I have to go, though. I have to save this Valentine's Day for him now," I half laugh.

"If I can do anything please let me know." She sounds like she means it. I want to tell her she's done enough, but I don't.

"Thanks. I'll talk to you later." I hang up the phone. What am I going to do now? An idea comes to mind and I start putting it into action.

Chapter 4

Nix

I did give everyone the day off today for Valentine's Day, but I decided to work. Alex said she had some things to handle so there was no point in hanging out around the house by myself. Especially when there is paperwork to do. Rachel does most of my clerical, but I like to handle the orders. I want to make sure it's all perfect.

My alarm on my phone goes off and tells me that it's five p.m. I haven't heard much from Alex all day. That is surprising. I just shrug it off to her being busy. It is tax season. I lock up the job site and drive home. I wonder what Alex thinks is going on. Will she be wondering if I have something planned? Will she be hurt when she discovers I didn't do anything?

The house looks dark when I pull into the driveaway. I wonder if she isn't home. Then I see her Jeep. Maybe she isn't feeling good again and called it an early night. I open the front door and an instant smell of jasmine hits my nose. That's my favorite scent. I notice the house is dark because jasmine scented candles are on the floor leading towards the back patio. I follow them, surprised at how much light they actually give off. I blow them out as I go because the last thing, I want is our home burning down. I open the patio door and see Alex standing next to a table set for two. There are tea lights all around the patio creating a beautiful atmosphere.

"What is going on?" I ask, baffled by the scene.

"Happy Valentine's Day." She walks towards me and that's when I notice the long red dress that fits her body like a glove she is wearing. It's sexy without being revealing. I then look down at myself. I am still in my work clothes, jeans and a plain t-shirt.

"I should go change." I start to turn around, trying to remember where my suit is when she grabs my hand.

"You're fine. This is for you." She motions to her dress. "And this is for us." She leads me over to the table. I notice the china plates, crystal glasses, and sterling silver silverware. This setup was a gift from her parents, but we never really used it. Alex and I were simple. We liked things easy and not too flashy. But tonight was the perfect time to use them.

"I still don't understand." I tell her as I take my seat.

"You always make sure I feel special on Valentine's Day. It's my turn now." She smiles at me and that smile makes me want to say forget all this and take her inside so I can show her how special she really is to me. But I tell my magic to calm down. She put a lot of work into this and it's not her thing so I need to let her have this moment. She claps her hands and then I hear music. Suddenly, a waiter and two men come out from the side of the house. The men are singing a love song in Italian. The waiter sets down two plates of our favorite dishes from Francisco's and fills our glasses with red wine. I just sit there and stare with my jaw dropped. After the men finish their song, Alex nods to them and they exit, leaving us to be alone again.

"Wow. How did you get them to do that?" I still can't believe she got the singers and waiter from the restaurant to be in our backyard.

"I called in a favor. I do the accounting for the restaurant. So, when I explained what I wanted to do the owner he was happy to help in exchange for me doing his taxes for free." She smiled and the warmth ran through my body.

"Thank you." I reach across the table and grab her hand. That's when I see a black box about the size of a greeting card. "What's this?"

"Open it," she tells me. I quickly grab the box and take off the lid. There is a folded-up piece of paper. I unfold it and read it. It's a medical report. Once the words sink in, I gasp. "Really?"

She nods with tears in her eyes. I can see the fear on her face. Fear that I might not want this. Now the way she acted after the doctor and her asking about kids makes sense. I get up from the table and kneel next to her.

****

Alex

When Nix gets up and comes over to kneel next to me, I swear my heart stops. What is he going to tell me? I know there is no way Nix won't be a good father. But I want this to be something he wants, not something he is thrown into. I look down at him and I see his watery eyes. I'm sure mine match. He places a hand over my stomach. The second he does I feel a small shock again.

"Alex, this is the most amazing gift you could ever give me." Tears are now apparent in his eyes. "Sure we didn't plan for this baby. But I want this baby. I want to be his or her father. And I want to have a family with you."

"Really?" I say through sobs I'm holding back.

"Of course. You are my life." He looks at my stomach. "And now so is this being."

"I love you, Nix," I tell him.

He raises up on his knees and grabs my face tenderly. "I love you, Alex." He kisses me and I swear I feel sparks like the first time we made love. His lips leave mine and already my lips miss him. "Let's enjoy this wonderful meal." He stands up and sits back down in his chair. We dive into the delicious dinner.

A few minutes later, Nix breaks the silence. "I can't believe you did all this. Especially with how you really feel about Valentine's Day. Why didn't you ever tell me?"

"I didn't want to hurt your feelings. You are so into it," I admitted, feeling embarrassed. It was silly that I never told him my feelings about the holiday.

"You usually have no problem telling me how you feel about things. Sometimes too boldly," he jokes and winks at me. I let out a laugh.

"I know. But this isn't a color I can't stand or a movie that annoys me. You always put so much work into giving us a special day, I'd hate to then tell you I really couldn't stand the holiday." I take a bite of my food.

Nix nods, understanding. "Well from now on let's be honest with each other." He looks around. "But for someone who doesn't like Valentine's Day, you did an amazing job." I smile at his compliment.

Once we finish, the waiter clears the plates and I thank him and tell him he can go home. "Did you want to call our parents and let them know the good news?" Nix asks, smiling at the piece of paper on the table.

I shake my head. "I want this to be our thing tonight." I stand up. "Besides, it's time for dessert."

"Didn't you just send the waiter home?" Nix states, not getting what I was meaning. I grab his hand and give him a seductive look. "Ohhh," he remarks, as it finally clicks. He lets me lead him into the house to end our celebration properly.

****

Nix

I can't sleep. I'm ecstatic. I am going to be a father. Alex and I are going to be parents. It's a scary thought, but also an exciting one. I know our parents are going to flip. My niece Abby is going to be an amazing cousin. Will we be raising a boy or girl? It doesn't matter. There are so many questions running through my head. Then the doubt comes in. Will I be a good parent? I hope I don't screw this child up.

"Go to sleep," Alex says to me. I look at her, surprised. Her eyes are still closed. I thought she was fast asleep. "I can hear your busy mind over here," she teases.

I chuckle. "I just can't believe we are going to be parents," I admit. She opens her eyes and smiles at me. "I can't help but feel nervous. What if I mess up?"

Alex sits up. "Nix, listen to me. You are going to be an amazing father. This child will learn so much from you. He or she doesn't know it yet, but it is so lucky that you are going to be its father. I mean it. I wouldn't want to start a family with anyone else."

"Thank you," I tell her and kiss her. Those were the words I needed to hear. Alex always knows exactly what I always need. This is why she is my everything.

"Goodnight," she lays back down. "Happy Valentine's Day."

"Happy Valentine's Day," I say back to her, before I shut my eyes.

Best Valentine's Day Ever.

Just One Night

A Just One Taste

Short Story

by

McKenzie Stark

Chapter 1

The velvet night shined with the promise of a new tomorrow and the stars kissed the endless darkened sky as it hung above. Beckoned by its serenade of its own creation- the telling of an even better future.

I watched from my apartment balcony, leaning against the railing. I smile, my hair brushed across my forehead with the light breeze. It's a beautiful night, that much I can say. The world that sat beneath me was lit by the rich colors of life, staring up at me with their own wide eyes. I never thought that things could get better, but somehow, I'd been wrong.

One sudden decision changed my life forever and while the path it took me was bumpy and let's face it, a bit emotional, filled with equal parts pleasure, pain and happiness. There's not a moment where I imagined doing anything differently. The actions I took, the decisions I made, it got me here. Right where I am today. Of course, I'd left town to take an offer outside of Austen Enterprises, but at the time, I wasn't thinking rationally and although I'd give anything to go back - I'm comfortable right where I am. Even if it meant never returning.

It hasn't been easy to say so the least. After my grandma was diagnosed with dementia and placed into care, I'd forced myself to carry on scoring a gorgeous apartment and working at the barista. Not the future I'd imagined for myself, but it was something. After my best friend, Jamie, strategically went behind my back and told my former boss and the man whose charm and wit won me over, to unknowingly force me to face him after that bitch Jessica wedged her crooked nose right into what could have been the best or the worse thing to ever happen to me. Of course, things happened to fall into place like a metal door and hearing Kaiden's confession that A. He did feel more than he'd lead on - thank god, I would have hated to be that girl, the one who falls for her boss who only wanted her for a quick lay., No matter how much he rocked my world. And B. That Kaiden Sloane. The sexy CEO of Austen Enterprises Magazine was a father. I was left to my own confused yet hopeful thoughts. And if that didn't surprise me all to hell. Then I don't know what would. That confounding night opened doors to a path that both scared and excited me. Kaiden being the man that he has always been had tried to persuade me into going back to NYC with him. I shot that down almost immediately. New York will always be my home. But being here in Nashville has opened new doors for me - although he would disagree with that. I was working at a coffee house after all.

The long night was spent wrapped in his arms while he whispered sweet nothing into my ear and when morning came, I walked him to the door and with a tender kiss that left me trembling. I watched him walk away. Right back to his high-end company and leaving me pondering what we would be doing right now had I made the decision to jump on the plane with him.

"A little too late for that," I mumbled into the dark.

Tomorrow is Valentine's day and the realization that I will spend it alone falls over me. My mood dampens at the thought and I let out a huff of air, hugging myself before shuffling inside. The heat of the fireplace kisses my skin as I settle onto the couch, pulling the book from my side table and indulging myself into it to wield my mind from the depressing thoughts of the inevitable Holiday.

It's never been my time of the year, not because I didn't have someone to spend it with, but because there was really no reason to. When growing up, it wasn't a Holiday that was strongly celebrated in my family, not even between my parents. Not that it really mattered, I was too little to really understand the concept of the entire day.

But now, I can't shake the small ache in my heart at the thought of spending the day alone and I don't know why.

I toss the book aside, unable to focus on the words before dragging myself towards my bedroom. It was late and I was more than ready to cuddle beneath my blankets and rid myself of this day all together. The darkness consumed me, wrapping me into its arms as the bitter cold rustled the window blinds. It kissed my bare skin and sent a shiver down my spine. The blankets do little to nothing to shield me from the blizzard outside my bedroom window and my teeth clatter together.

The thoughts are still somersaulting inside of my head, but it doesn't take long before my body's will to fight sleep is lost and I am thrown into my own unconscious mind.

Chapter 2

Upon waking, I burrow myself deeper into the comfort of my blankets, shielding the morning light from my already raging headache. The sound of my phone buzzing on my nightstand causes a groan to escape my parted lips. Who could possibly be calling me at this hour?

My eyes still shut as I soak in the cool air, letting my muscles awaken from their slumber. The moment my phone silences, it erupts again, but this time from an incoming call.

With a long exhale, I reluctantly peel my eyes open instantly regretting it as the bitter light nearly blinds me. I blink, squeezing my eyes closed before reopening them and taking in the snow that drifts from the mouth of the sky from my window.

I rub the back of my knuckles to my eyes, riding them of the last restraints of my sleep. My eyes fall on my phone and against my better judgement, I slide my legs off the side of the bed, planting my bare feet against the floor, stretching my arms above my head.

Muffling a yawn I swipe my phone off the table and peer at the screen. It appears my best friend didn't get the memo that I would like to enjoy this day wallowing in my own loneliness. I shake my head, before bringing the phone to my ear.

The static on the other side breaks as her voice comes on, "Kaira, there you are! I have been trying to reach you all morning,"

"Sorry," I replied, not at all aroused with excitement.

"Please tell me you're not seriously lounging around in your bed, still in your pajamas?" Jamie lets out a loud sigh.

"Of course, not."

Lie.

"Are you sure?" she asked.

I press my lips together, pulling myself up and shuffling over to the balcony. "I am not lounging in my bed, Jamie."

Only a partial lie.

"It's Valentines, Kaira."

"I am very much aware," I tell her.

She clicks her tongue, before responding, "You don't sound so thrilled at the idea."

It wasn't like I hadn't expected my best friend to hound me about enjoying this day, but I can't help the pang of anger that rushes through me. She knows exactly why today isn't my cup of tea, and still she expects me to quiver in excitement. Like I'm not in another State, far from my friends with nothing to do but wallow in my own space.

"You know how I feel about Valentines," I remind her, running a hand over my face.

The cool air bites at my skin when I prop the sliding door open, stepping out onto the snow-covered balcony and breathing in the fresh air.

Jamie doesn't drop the issue as easily as I would have hoped she would have. "Yeah, I do and normally I would be all for lounging around with a bowl of chocolate and crying to sappy love stories with you, darling. But that was before you have a complete hunk as a boyfriend. You should be jumping fucking ecstatic right now."

"A boyfriend who is not here," I begin, a smile tugging at my lips. The thought of Kaiden being mine does nothing to stop the rush of blood that kisses my cheeks or the trumpet of my heart racing beneath my chest. "It's not like I have anything better to do."

There's a smile in Jamie's voice when she speaks, "Have I ever let you down?"

"Well, no. But -"

"No buts. Get your petite ass up off whatever furniture you've claimed as your hibernation and get in the shower," There was a no arguing tone to her voice and I shook mine, all but ready to shoot her idea down. "Oh! And where something nice," She replied.

Against my will, my feet drag me across the floor and into the bathroom, "Fine."

"Hurry up," she pauses, "And don't think about disconnecting the call, either. I know what you're thinking Kaira and you're not getting out of this."

I roll my eyes, letting out a huff of air, "Whatever." The phone rests on the countertop as I move to climb beneath the smoldering hot water.

It kissed my skin, stinging but in a good way. I duck my head beneath it, closing my eyes. I was in no hurry to get out, but with my friends constantly nagging to hurry my ass up, I rushed to scrub my aching muscles before dragging myself out and tossing on a pair of clothes, rinsing my hair out with the towel before looking at myself in the mirror.

The face staring back at me is lined with disagreement and I can't help the small chuckle that sneaks its way out at my own appearance.

"Care to enlighten me on what's got you all giggly over there?" Jamie's voice comes over the voice.

"Nope," I tease, smiling despite myself. "Why aren't you out doing something?"

I could already picture the scowl and lift of her shoulder on the other side of the phone. "Because I, for one, don't have to be bribed into enjoying themselves for once," she points out.

The buzzer on my door sounds and my eyes dart towards the bedroom, as though I could see through the thick walls into whoever is on the other side of my door.

"Who could possibly be here?" I grumble, running a hand through my damp hair.

"Why don't you go check?" Jamie asked, her voice hitching.

There was a delicious moment when everything around me fell into a complete blur, like the room diminished into thin air and all that was there in the moment was my eyes locked on his and my entire insides tingled with an electricity that leaves me frozen with my hand still wrapped around the door handle.

He smiles, the one that makes my heart skip a beat, and Jamie's voice is left forgotten as the phone hangs at my side, stuck in my grip.

Words completely left me, I stared into those eyes and my heart and soul fell silent. My mouth opens but the words betray me, only to slam it shut as I swallow the knot in my throat. The tears are already welling up in my eyes and I can't stop them as they break free, trailing down my cheeks. The rush of happiness that falls over me in that moment is almost too much to grasp onto as I step back, phone falling with a THUD against the floor as my hands cup over my mouth.

"Kaiden?" I breathe, my words that of a whisper.

The smile painted across his ungodly gorgeous features widens into a full-on grin. "Happy Valentine's day."

The sound of his voice kisses over my spine and sends goosebumps over my skin, "What...," I take a deep breath. "What are you doing here?"

"I couldn't leave my girl to celebrate the Holiday alone, now could I?" he asked, standing before me in the most perfect suit, black and occupied by a red tie that does nothing to stop my mind from wandering to all the things he could be using it for. In his hand, he holds a boutique of roses that makes my heart clench.

His girl.

God, I will never get over the sound of that.

Without further ado. I am flinging myself into her welcoming arms, burying my head into the nook of his neck and breathing him in. Kaidens arms encircle my waist, drawing me nearer, his chin rests on top of my head.

I have never felt so much at once, but fuck did the emotions wreck into me like a storm. "I can't believe you're here."

"I wouldn't miss it for the world," he whispers into my hair.

I pull back, staring up at him. "I missed you."

Kaiden leans forward, his fingers glazing over my hips. "I missed you, too," he said, right before he covers the distance between us.

The brush of his lips gliding against my own is almost too much to take and not enough at all, I press forward, deepening the kiss as my arms fall around his neck, fingers tangling into his short hair. His tongue darts out, silently asking for permission and I grant it. Our tongues move in sync, a silent dance as they fight for dominance. I let Kaiden take the lead, my body tingling with every brush of his lips desperately against my own, hungrily. He held me by the waist pulling me into him until our bodies were one, pressed firmly together. A sound escapes between his lips, something between a growl and a groan and it shoots a surge of need to my core. I almost whimper at the sound alone, holding back as I move the angle of the kiss to draw his lip between my own. It was like a million stars erupted around us, fireworks going off. God, how I had missed this.

When Kaiden left that night, it took everything in me not to run after him, but now - in this moment, I wouldn't have changed it for the world. Because if I could have a million of these moments, these surprise encounters that leave me both breathless and itching for me - then why the hell not?

Kaiden pulled back, moving his hands to cup my face while he gazed into my eyes with the most sincere and loving gleam. He runs his thumbs across the base of my jaw, resting his forehead against my own.

"You have no idea how long I've wanted to do that," he confessed, drawing a smile to my face.

"I can say the same."

So many thoughts condensed into that very moment. The sound of Jamie's muffled voice draws me from my high, reluctantly pulling away, I swoop down and retrieve the phone from where I had dropped it.

"Hello!" Jamie yells, an annoyed but playful edge to her voice. "I swear, if you two are getting it on while I am on the phone, I am going to make sure you both pay for this."

I chuckle, "Stop your worrying. We are both fully clothed."

"Thank god!" she replies. "I was beginning to worry."

"You and I both know that you were far from worrying Jamie."

"I don't know what you're talking about."

"Oh?" I ask, eyes darting towards Kaiden as he makes his way towards the kitchen. Oh man did he have a nice ass! I shake the thoughts before focusing my attention back to my rambling friend.

Jamie was in the middle of a rant, only catching the last half of it, "I will have you know. So before you go on about thinking I had something to do with this," she states, "I would rethink it, sweetheart."

"Did you?"

"Did I what?" Jamie asked, rant over.

I move towards the kitchen, resting my ass against the counter, eyes focused on Kaiden while he works to get the flowers into a vase that is non-existent in my place - I watch with an arched brow as he settles for a cup.

Jamie continues, "Earth to Kaira."

"What?" I ask, slightly distracted that Kaiden was in my place, again and how ungodly he looked. "Sorry."

"Uh huh," she drawls. "Did I what?"

"Have anything to do with it?"

There was a pause and a ruffle of clothing before Jamie replied, "Yes. I might have had a little bit to do with it."

"Exactly."

"Oh shut up, you know you love me for it."

I smile, shaking my head despite myself. "Of course I do, you dork."

Kaiden turns to look at me, his eyes dark. He steps forward, brushing a piece of my hair behind my ear, fingers glazing over my cheek. "Hey Jamie?" There was no way I was going to stay on the phone a moment longer as long as Kaiden was standing in front of me. "Can I call you later?"

"You better get some hot smoldering sex tonight if you're trying to push me off the phone already!"

"Jamie," I began, playing with the red tie around Kaidens neck, eyes never swaying from his, "What I do or do not do tonight is for me to know and for you..." The words fall short as Kaiden arms wrap around me, his hands gripping firmly against my ass as he holts me upward and onto the counter before stepping in between my legs.

He gives me a cocky smirk, prying the phone from my hand. Not that it took much for me to give it up. I watch as he places it to his ear, "Jamie, she's going to have to call you back. Stay out of trouble." He states, ending the call he slides it into his pack pocket before his hands fall against my thighs.

Kaiden leans forward, his lips trailing across my neck. I edge my head to the side to allow him more space, closing my eyes against the rush of ecstasy. My hands grip his tie tighter, pulling him closer. Just when I think my heart is going to burst from my chest, my cheeks flushing, whether from the cool air that fills the apartment or the close proximity of Kaiden I am not sure. He pulls back planting a chaste kiss to my waiting lips.

"You're just as beautiful as ever," He says.

The depth of his words cut deeper than ice and I have not a doubt that he means every word. How can one person be so perfect?

"I can't believe you're here."

Kaiden smiles. "Did you really think that I would leave you here alone, especially on a day like this?"

"I don't know." I lift a shoulder in response. Of course, I had thought that. It wasn't like Kaiden wasn't a CEO of a large Company who requires a large portion of his attention. I worked there, I know that it's hard to get any leave time and if you did, it wasn't much.

Well, he is the CEO Kaira. He can do what he wants.

I begin, twiddling my thumbs. "I don't particularly like this day. If I am being honest."

"Why is that?"

"Valentines is full of sappy people in love, who think they need a specific day to show the person they care about how much they mean to them." I bite my lip, watching him from under my lashes. "It just doesn't sound appealing to me."

"We'll see about that," he decides. "I'm going to show you that there is more to this day than that. And when I do, you'll be thanking me for showing up on your doorstep."

"You can show up on my doorstep anytime."

Kaiden reaches for my hand, entwining our fingers, "Good to know." He moves to lift me off the counter, feet back on the ground he gives my hand a gentle squeeze, "Come on, we have some shopping to do."

I scowl, but follow after him. It doesn't take long for us to arrive at the store, Kaiden dragging me swiftly behind him as his long legs take him through each aisle. He moves with ease, throwing stuff into the cart, his hand wrapped in my own the entire time. It felt so natural, being like this with him. We never did this, at least not outside of work - to think of it, we've never been like this at all. It was always sex with us and fuck was the sex amazing.

But to be standing here, in the open with him with no fear of being caught or judged that an intern was sleeping with her boss. It felt normal and I could allow myself to get used to it - bathe in it really. I step forward, dropping his hand only to wrap mine around her arm. He gazes down at me with a curve of his lips, leaning downward to place a kiss on my forehead, we continue through the store.

I couldn't help how my heart grows bigger with every step, each gentle look and smile he tosses my way. I am completely captivated by Kaiden in so many ways.

Chapter 3

After spending a good twenty minutes trying to convince Kaiden that if he was going to make me endure this tortuous Holiday, ice cream was a must - we made our way towards the check out. The ride back to my apartment was almost endless, until the large building finally came into view. The minute his car stopped I jumped from the passenger side seat, throwing the back door open and filling my arms with bags. Ignoring his attempt to take the majority of them while tossing him a wink over my shoulder, I head inside.

"You're so stubborn," he grumbles, as he holds the door open, allowing me to step through.

"Don't act like you don't like it," I tease him, setting the bags on the counter.

Kaiden shakes his head. "Why don't you go pick a movie and I'll get dinner started?"

"Okay." I place a kiss on his cheek and stride into the living room, falling back against the couch and sinking into the cushions. "What are you in the mood to watch?"

"Maybe one of those chick flicks, you know the ones where the girl gets what she wants?" he began, his tone teasing, I laughed at his attempt at being funny.

I click away at the remote, channel by channel flashing across the small TV. "Yeah, because that's what you want to watch," I reply sarcastically, rolling my eyes.

The sweet aroma of food hits my nose and my stomach grumbles in response. The smell intoxicating and I can't help but peer over my shoulder, waiting patiently was never my cup of tea. Especially, when it involves food, but Kaiden chuckles upon seeing my eager eyes and dishes the food out, making himself a place beside me on the couch.

I don't waste any time wolfing down the delicious food, barely tasting a thing in my hurry to settle the ache in my stomach. Upon my last bite, I give him a sideways glance, slightly embarrassed about not being very woman-like in that moment, but Kaiden doesn't look in the least bit offended, focusing on devouring his own plate.

The movie I'd settled on was some comedy that left us both chuckling around mouths full of food. Although my previous attempts of Valentine's still remain untangled. I can't deny that Kaidens company has brightened the entire day and suddenly the Holiday didn't seem all that bad.

I push my plate away, stomach full and hunger quenched. Unconsciously, I lean further into Kaidens embrace, cuddling into his side. He drops an arm around my shoulder, glazing his fingers over my bare arm. A shiver runs down my spine and I close my eyes at the sensual sensation that's always occupied this man's touch. Kaiden drops a kiss to my head, pulling me closer against him.

There wasn't a moment that I didn't want to spend in his world, wrapped snuggly in the close proximity of each other. Or, getting lost in those steamy eyes that have a way of stealing my breath away.

"Have I changed your outlook on Valentine's day, yet?" Kaiden asked, nudging my side with a knowing smile.

I cast him an astute gaze, not ready for him to know that he has, in fact, altered my thoughts on this particular day, "I may be open to the idea of indulging in it. *If* it means spending it with you," I began, tossing him a wink for good measures.

The sound of his laugh melts my heart and I watch him with lovestruck eyes. "Is that right?" he asked, lips curling upward.

I shrug, "What can I say?" My hands find refugee against her side, fingers playing with the hem of his shirt. "You have a way of changing my mind."

"In that case." Kaidens lips brush against the sensitive spot on my neck, sending a fire through my veins. I tilt my head to allow him more access, "I have a few other ideas on how to change your mind."

"I think I might like to know what other ideas are," I breathe, eyes fluttering closed.

Kaiden hums against my neck.

The thought turns my mind to mush, occupied by the sweet enticing brush of his fingers against my side does wicked things to me. My heart thumps wildly inside my chest like drumsticks beating against my ribs.

I never could get over the feelings Kaiden was able to bring out in me. It always left me longing for more. I never thought I could feel so much for someone, but he changed that for me. If you would have asked me where I saw myself - wrapped in my former bosses arms on one of the most romantic nights of the year - would not have been it.

But fuck did it feel good. In this moment, I didn't have to pretend that my feelings weren't intensifying every second I sat wrapped in his arms. I wouldn't want to be anywhere else, because we were twin flames burning like an inferno of a thousand fires.

The gut-wrenching bang that pours through the open window draws me from my thoughts and the comfort of Kaidens embrace. Right before the apartment is engulfed in darkness.

"Shit!" I reluctantly pull away from Kaiden, eyes squinting against the darkened room.

"Hold on," he states, moving towards the closet, "I'll grab some candles."

I let out a huff of air, "I'll be right here." My eyes adjusting to the newfound light, "It's not like I have anywhere better to be."

Kaiden laughs, "It's just a little power outage, Kaira."

"One that is successfully ruining our night."

Unable to remain still, I busy myself with removing the dishes from the table, shuffling towards the kitchen and dumping them dramatically into the sink. I know I probably shouldn't be so upset, but I haven't seen Kaiden in months, separated by distance and this is how fate repays me.

"Stupid Holiday," I mumble to the bare walls hugged around me, pulling the fridge open I snatch the container of chocolate covered strawberries from the top shelve. Of course, I don't leave the kitchen without the carton of ice cream, my poor heart wouldn't like me very much if I had.

Chapter 4

The living room is twinkling with the small glow of the candles that Kaiden managed to spread across the room, giving it a sense of comfort and warmth.

He's kneeled beside the fireplace, poking away at the small, ignited flame he'd managed to get sizzling, when I return. He peers over his shoulder with a charming smile. "What you got there?"

I hold up the contents in my hand, waving them teasingly. "I figured we could eat away our disappointment."

"Who says I'm disappointed?" he asked, arching a brow.

"Why wouldn't you be, the dreadful weather was successful at ruining our movie." My hands fall against my waist, cocking my hip out as I wait for him to respond.

Kaiden looks at me with amusement before turning back to the fire, poking it with the poker and pulling himself to his feet once he feels satisfied.

He moves across the room, eyes trained on me and I can feel the heat of them beating against my bare skin, my breath hitches as he speaks. "You weren't even into it. Don't think I didn't notice you watching me."

My cheeks blush a scarlet red. Of course, I'd been watching him out of the corner of my eye, but how could

I not? It still felt so surreal that he was standing in front of me and I couldn't get enough of it.

"Maybe that's true, but you're much more fun to look at." I grin, feeling pleased with myself.

Kaiden falls to a stop before me, his eyes full of tempting suggestions that has me biting the inside of my cheek. "You're something else," he says, reaching forward to run the tips of his fingers down my arm, shuddering in response my knees threaten to buckle. "It never fails to amaze me."

My fingers itch to reach forward and draw him closer. The space between us far too much. But as Kaidens fingers glaze against my knuckles, I hold my breath. But what he does next leaves me both trembling with annoyance and wanting to flick him in the ear.

He never takes his eyes off my own, his fingers wrapping around my hand and driving me completely bonkers. That is until he pulls away with the containers that once rested in my grip. And with a smartass smirk over his shoulder he moves towards the couch. Leaving me to my own tangled thoughts.

I scowl, shaking my head. "That was evil."

"It's never bothered you before," he points out, patting the space beside him, "Now get your gorgeous ass over here."

"Yes sir,. I roll my eyes.

"I have something for you," he says, reaching into his back pocket revealing a folded piece of paper.

I arch a brow, "What is it?"

"Why don't you open it and find out?" he asks, holding the paper loosely between his fingers.

Curious, I don't hesitate to take it, peeling it open to find neatly placed words, nestled between the straight lines. I peer up at him under my lashes before clearing my throat, letting my eyes soak them in. My heart aching with so many emotions, face softening.

A love letter.

Kaiden wrote me a love letter, and although the paper is tattered and wrinkled, the words fall against my once tangled soul, coursing through my veins and springing tears to my eyes.

The words fall off the paper like a 3D movie, jumping out at me with so much love that my heart grows larger.

Love.

Fuck how those three words hang on the tip of my tongue. But given our past mistakes, I find myself unable to spill them openly and freely. No matter how much my heart wishes me to.

I look up at him, wiping at my eyes. "What is this?" My voice cracks.

He reaches forward, capturing a tear with his thumb, his hand resting against my cheek. I lean into his touch. "It's everything I want to say but can't find the right words to say it."

Kaiden kisses the tears away, brushing my hair back from my face. "You're everything to me," he continues. "I never thought that one person could make me feel this way, but you managed to break through my walls and I couldn't be luckier to call you mine."

I let out a breathy laugh, sniffling. "Who knew you could be such a sap."

Kaiden smiles, "I guess you bring it out in me."

"Something we both can agree on."

He watches me in silence, as though he were contemplating something before he speaks, "Come back."

"What?"

"I want you to come back home."

"You know I can't do that," I tell him. "We've already had this conversation."

Kaiden frowns. "Kaira, I know you feel obligated to stay here. I understand." I know that wasn't the end of the discussion, so I remain silent, "But don't you think Jamie would like her best friend back? You could come back to Austen Enterprises, you know there's always a place there for you."

"I can't." It wasn't that I didn't want to, because it has crossed my mind once or twice. But the thought of going back, after being away so long. It terrified me.

I open my mouth to speak, only for Kaiden to raise a finger to stop any excuse tumbling from my lips, I slam my mouth closed. "You can," he insists, pulling my hand into his own he brings it to his lips placing a chaste kiss to my knuckles, "Jamie needs you... I *need* you. I can't do this without you Kaira. It's not just about the company. There isn't a moment that I don't want to spend with you at my side. I want to be able to hold you at night and wake to your beautiful smile. I want you to argue with me about what is right or wrong for the company and test my patience. I want to see you and not stress the added miles between us."

"I want you," Kaiden says, the sincere look in his eyes tells me that he means every word.

The winckled and ink-stained love letter wrapped in my hand, I stare into his eyes and my lips move on their own accord, "Okay."

"Okay?" he asks, eyes searching my own.

I give him a small smile, "Yes. I'll come back. But only if *I* tell Jamie on my own terms."

Before I knew it, Kaidens slid his hands to my thighs, lifting me effortlessly onto his lap and devouring my face in kisses. I laugh, lightly pushing at his shoulders, "Kaidennn!"

"You don't know how happy that makes me," he says against my ear.

"I think I have a pretty good idea," I say, placing a kiss against his cheek. "Now can we please indulge ourselves in some sweet goodness, already?"

Amused, Kaiden holds a strawberry between us, "Open up," the way his voice sounds huskier than before, and the innuendo behind his words sends an ache to my core that has me pressing my thighs together. From my place across his lap, I can only hope he doesn't notice how sexually frustrated I had become.

He holds the strawberry to my lips and I take a bite, the sweet taste latching onto my taste buds, "Mmm," I moan, closing my eyes, "That's delicious."

Kaiden laughs, "You have a little -" he shakes his head. "Here, let me," his finger brushes against the edge of my mouth. I grab his wrist, drawing his finger into my mouth, sucking. He takes a sharp intake of air.

My tongue darts out, running across my bottom lip. Kaiden watches it with darkened eyes, misted with desire, "You're playing with fire, Kaira."

I lean toward, my lips a mere inches from his own, "Maybe I want to get burned."

Kaiden growls, leaning forward he captures my lips between his own. And fuck if I didn't come undone in that moment. The night was spent lovemaking beneath the starry sky, blanketed in the fiery glow of candles and wrapped in each other's arms until our bodies had grown spent from the utter bliss that the other drew out. It was unlike any night I had ever experienced and I knew, without a doubt, I wanted to experience every Holiday with Kaiden. And I wanted to do it in the comfort surroundings of the place my heart desires.

Because Kaiden Sloane is my home.

And home was exactly where I needed to be.

Love Language

A Girl Named Flower

Short Story

by

Shawna Hunter

Chapter 1

Love is in the air. Well, actually the smell of fresh baked chocolate macaroons is in the air, but what else would love smell like? I mean, aside from leather and sweat. That sort of love will come later tonight, though. For now, I have a domestic little girlfriend in the kitchen. Abeba, dark skin and shaved head, supple breasts wrapped in emerald green lace. The matching thong barely visible on that sexy butt, until she bends over. My Abeba. The girl I turned my life upside down for. Every inch of her presented, just as I love to see it. My reward for the risks I took and the things I did to keep her safe. Abeba loves to tease and taunt. She knows I'm watching. I am always watching her. A reporter by trade, I am Mrs. Observant and Abeba helps me keep my keen edge. With no tongue, she communicates more with body and sign language than with words. She can speak, to an extent, but she prefers not to. Abeba doesn't like the sound of her words. I, however, think they are the most beautiful sounds in the world.

Today, she's focused on telling me one thing, how much she loves me. February 14th. A silly tradition, but Abeba loves silly traditions. The housewife, the submissive, the loving supporter. I think it has something to do with how non-traditional a couple we happen to be. An Asian-American New York girl and an

Ethiopian runaway living, unmarried, as an interracial lesbian couple. In a small town secretly full of BDSM enthusiasts, no less. With all that on our plate, and the memories of recent events fresh in the back of our minds, it's no wonder that she'd want something simple. Like baking macaroons for her lover on Valentine's Day. Not that I'll indulge her for long. Domesticity is Abeba's love language. Mine is a little more direct. Take, for example, my decree that she wear nothing but lingerie today, or my rule that she is not to leave the house. No friends, no dinners out, no getting away. A complete lockdown, with her dominatrix girlfriend. I watch as she takes the treats from the oven, offering me a view of that cute butt. Patiently, I wait until she places them on the windowsill to cool. She smells them as I tiptoe towards her, she seems pleased with the results. I know she knows I'm coming. Abeba always knows, and never resists. When my hand slides down her arm to pin her hand to the counter, a tiny smile curls her lips. She was expecting this. Such a good girl.

"Bending over a counter." I allow her other hand to move from the sill to the counter, "is asking for it."

She nods, pressing her hips out. There's no doubt as to what's coming, and Abeba knows just how I like her positioned. So sexy, so clever. Every one of our friends has asked why I haven't, yet, put a ring on her finger or a collar around her neck. I don't really know myself. I've purchased both, I just keep putting it off. It will happen, of course, but not today. Abeba would appreciate the tradition, but I wouldn't be able to stomach the cliche. So, she'll just have to content herself with the spanking. There will be plenty of life ahead to have her kneeling at the altar. Yes, when we've discussed it, I've made that demand. Flowers, music, choice of cake are hers, but the ceremony will have her kneeling at my side. Traditional? No, but if she wants me to make a spectacle of myself in front of our friends then, damn it, I'll make it a spectacle of the real me. For now, however, there's just her ass and my thin, cool hands.

You've got to turn your wrist as you strike. That's the secret to a good spanking. It's not a sharp slap, that'll just cause bruising. What you really want is to make the ass cheek lift up a little. The shaking looks cute, of course, but the deep thud of it makes the body react. After the first few strikes, I squeeze. I can feel her heartbeat, the throbbing sensation pumping warmth and tingles through her. That's blood flow, moving to swell and cushion the area. The body's defense mechanism, and one which carries a delightful side benefit. The same arteries that pump the blood to her heart shaped butt, also connect to her sweet little pussy. She can't help the arousal. That's how the body does it. Pumping blood to the sex organs. I'm just moving things along as I assert my dominance. Abeba, is putty in my hands. When my hand slides down her body, it dips between her thighs. Wet, hot, things are proceeding exactly as planned. She trembles slightly when I open

244

the drawer. What will I use? The rubber spatula may be a bit too harsh. The cutting board is tempting, but the wooden spoon is just too traditional to pass up.

"I hope your mommy never did this," I tease, as I tap her. Abeba's mother was a prostitute. She had barely been able to support Abeba. My girl learned her life lessons on the streets, conning and manipulating to stay alive. Eventually she found and blackmailed her biological father. Now, she's in a nice house getting spanked in her own kitchen. A true success story, for a submissive. Abeba bites her lips with the first few swats. Those thick, luscious lips of hers that make me want to stop and kiss her. I don't, however, not yet. Like waiting on the macaroons until after dinner, I leave the kisses until she's had a proper spanking. I know it's starting to hurt. Her hands close into fists as her eyes flutter shut. Having an orgasm, without permission, will get her punished, but that's not what she's afraid of. Abeba doesn't, usually, cum from spanking alone. What she's afraid of, is getting me to stop. Abeba has a safe word. Like any good, kinky couple. The problem is that Abeba must speak hers, out loud. No signing it allowed. Cruel, I know, but you have to understand that Abeba's voice is magical. It freezes me, every time. Like having Cupid's arrow strike me in the throat. Besides, Abeba loves my cruelty. More so when it's directed at others, but you don't date a demon and then complain when you get poked by the horns.

"Sop," she gasps at last. It's as close as she can get to "stop." It sounds more like "hop" but she manages to contort the "h" sound just enough. It's one of those silly, mutilated words forced by her lack. One of the words she hates, so I know she's truly had enough when she resorts to it.

Theatrically, I place the spoon on the counter, next to her hand. I have stopped, as requested, but that doesn't mean we're done. I massage her, groping and squeezing to help ease the throbbing and move all that blood along. She's warm now, I can smell her arousal. A slight musk, beneath the scent of the macaroons, that makes my mouth water. Self-control is key. The domme can have what she wants, when she wants it...unless the sub says "no." That does not, however, mean that she should. If I have Abeba now, then dinner will be late and all of my plans for tonight will be rearranged. We'll end up tired and sluggish, may even miss the main course. So, I have to back myself away from her, and hold myself back when she turns towards me. With one arched eyebrow she asks me for more, offers her body to me. I have to be the one to hit the brakes, slow things down. The burdens of power.

"You're such a good girl," I tell her, "so sexy and strong. So wet, too," I point towards the front of her thong. She grinds her thighs just a little, before parting them. Showing me that little emerald triangle and the promise of what lies beneath. "Not yet, Flower," I tease her with my pet name for her, "you still have to cook me

246

dinner remember?" She drops her chin, pouting in a last-ditch attempt to tempt me, "get to work."

Chapter 2

Dinner tonight, will be a slow cooked whole chicken with mashed potatoes, green beans and Mimosas. Abeba, ever the culinary hobbyist, wanted to try something more complex. I, however, had put my foot down. I selected this meal because of its cooking time. Plenty of time to toy with the chef while the meal slowly reaches perfection. Besides, my Flower won't be able to touch herself while peeling potatoes or seasoning chicken. Not if she's smart. We like our food spicy and you don't want chilli powder on your sensitive areas. Not after the last time Abeba ticked me off, she won't be forgetting that any time soon. No, she's a good girl. She'll have to work while horny and unsatisfied. Work to please me, so I'll reward her. Work to show her love for me, which I've never doubted. I watch her, of course, how can I not? As she turns to get to work, I have to make fists with my toes. Make no mistake, I want to ravage her. I just know better.

She signs at me that I'm a bitch...and a distraction. I know it's true. I'm practically radiating my desire for her. Her lingerie accents her dark, curvy body. My own clothing teases her with what I have to offer. A sheer black T-shirt that hints at the bare nipples below. A knee length skirt that meets my knee-high boots. Her hands fly through the air, begging me to wait in the living room. I comply, turning slowly as I feel her eyes on me. My hands move to the skirt, lifting it slowly to reveal my snow-white, bare ass before I flip the skirt back down and strut out. No bra, no panties. Nothing but goodies to be unwrapped by Abeba, if and when I allow her to do so. The smells from the kitchen follow me into the living room. Beckoning me to the sight of Abeba prancing around. There's no need for television, not with a fresh spanked chef, putting on a show for me. I plop myself down in a lounger, where I can curl my hands behind my head and watch her. Tempting her to glance over and see me, and everything I have to offer.

For thirty minutes, I watch her steal glances at me. There's no reason to blame her, I'm not ashamed to admit that even I am turned on by me. I feel sexy, powerful, especially as I stroke the little chest on the end table to my right. A jewellery box, of sorts, the first birthday present Abeba ever got me. She told me then that an evil queen needs a place to store those hearts. Abeba is a dream. Slow, careful. Everything she does, right down to the smallest detail, has to be perfect for me. If she finds a green bean that stands out from the rest, she discards it. If a potato doesn't peel just right, off it goes. Even seasoning the chicken. She doesn't just sprinkle it. Every inch has to be done just right. No shortcuts, no mistakes. I wouldn't have been surprised to see her pull out a ruler, but she knows better than to tempt me like that. Finally, I hear the timer being set. The chicken will take the longest. Abeba will have it timed so that it's second seasoning will take place just before it's time to mash the potatoes. Then they'll warm with the green beans as the chicken completes. With all her cooking blogs, I haven't been able to help picking up a thing or two. Which gives me the perfect window.

"Come here pet," I say, when I know she'll have nothing to do. "I want to play with you some more."

My Flower doesn't lilt as she enters. The heat from the oven has caused a slight sheen to her body, it makes the emerald lace cling. My breath catches for a moment as I study her. The bra is sheer enough to get a sense of the breasts beneath. It lifts them, presenting them in a way that is, admittedly, unnatural but visually appealing. The thong has more fabric in its 3 straps than it has covering her clean-shaven sex. Just a little sliver of green, barely enough to hide the pink below. Abeba wanted pink or red lingerie. She wanted candy hearts all over her body and red ribbons tying her hands. I told her we could do that after Valentine's day. When all that commercial crap was on sale. I wanted the contrast of green against her dark skin. "Giving me what I want," I'd whispered in her ear, "is the best way for you to say that you love me." Abeba had had no response but compliance, once I'd told her that. How can I not be in love with this girl?

"Kneel," I tell her, as my hand strokes the box, she gave me. The contents are ever changing, nothing within matters as much as the gift itself, "show me your breasts."

The advantage to the sheer lace push-up is the ease with which it can be pulled down. It's certainly not something I make Abeba wear for comfort or support. Her hands slide up, luxuriating in the feel of the lace as she peels the front down, letting her nipples spill forth. Thick, swollen and ringed by areola darker than the surrounding skin. Abeba keeps her eyes down, she knows better than to glance up at me in this position. No pleading for compliments, no peaking for a hint of what I'll do to her. I asked for her breasts and here they are. My two fingers barely touch the skin. I can see the effect of that feather touch as I coax her nipples to attention. She inhales the second the clamps come into her view. By then, it's already too late. Butterfly clamps were a big seller, back when Abeba and I ran a little sex shop in the city. Not, as many mistakenly thought, clamps with little butterflies hanging from them but a clamp with a lower-case y shape beneath the handle. These devilish delights don't just pinch and tease, but they bite harder when pulled on. Tightening until they pop off.

Left, then right, my finger sliding down the chain connecting them and wrapping slowly, lifting and slowly pulling. Abeba can't help but arch her back as her nipples are pulled forward. I have her breasts wrapped around my finger. Most can imagine the pain, but few understand the tingle until they experience it. That strange, deep vibration that works its way back into your heart. There's always a reason other than simple pain. True pain sluts are very rare, but there are many who like a good nipple clamp. Abeba would have had a third clamp as well. One that reached lower, between those thighs of hers, but there would be no point. Not after the other horror those bastards had inflicted upon my Flower. Not a subject I want to dwell on, however, not now. Abeba and I have long since learned to work around that impediment, claiming all the pleasures that evil men once tried to deny her.

"No Flower," I say as her hands rise, "move those again and I'll cuff you." My free hand gently picks the thumb cuffs up from the chest. A small metal rectangle with two loops and a lock. These are much easier to store and conceal but just as effective as their big brothers. Slipping wrist cuffs is a trick many submissive learn. Slipping thumb cuffs isn't much harder. Slipping both? Well, dommes learn as many tricks for keeping a submissive in bondage as they learn for slipping out. It's all a part of the games we play.

Abeba doesn't want the cuffs. They'd make it so much harder to finish dinner, not to mention that they'd take her communication away. It's hard to sign around the chain, but Abeba manages it. She asks to touch herself. I refuse her.

"No, Flower, not yet. For now, you just be my good little toy." I can't fight the smile as she places her hands behind her butt and sits up, just a little taller.

I tug on the chain until the buzzer sounds. Just toying with her as she moans on her knees before me. There's no more to it than that. She, the center of my whole world and I the cause of her pleasurable torment. Abeba is wobbly as she gets to her feet. I leave the bra pulled down, the chain dangling from her nipples. Her ass bobs and sways as she makes her way back to the kitchen. Still, there's no rushing or cutting corners. The potatoes are mashed and whipped with deliberate care. The green beans watched like a hawk. When it's time to carve the chicken, she does so with surgical precision. Not a single stray bone, except on the leg. A half chicken dinner with fixings that she carefully plates as I attend to my contribution. I mix the drinks. After years of flirting with bartenders for leads, I've picked up a few things. Orange juice and sparkling wine. Proper orange juice, of course, pulp free but organic. Rich flavor and not too sweet. For the wine, I go for a sparkling Bartenura Moscato. A sweet Italian vintage that has very little alcohol. I want Abeba happy, not drunk. This is a night I want her to remember in every vivid detail.

Chapter 3

We sit across the table from one another. My foot lazily dragging up and down her leg. There are candles, of course, she needed some nod to tradition. I look at her, that coy little smile as her knife works. The chain, dangling from her clamps, shaking slightly. She's trying not to laugh. I'm trying not to compose a sonnet. Each bite of food is savored, each dish complimented. I know how hard she worked, how much it matters to her. Her thank you come in little blinks, shy smiles. At one point she brushes her hand over her ear. Once, before we'd had to run, she'd had long dreadlocks framing her face. When they'd come undone, she had had a corona of wild frizz which she hated. I didn't care, if it was hers, I loved it. Although, to be fair, the dreadlocks were more useful for bondage. The shaved head, however, had been necessary in our flight. Hiding out from assassins requires changing your look. Since that incident, Abeba had been growing it in but she still had only a slight fuzz. It's not hard at all to remember that night in our old bathroom, as I'd carefully shaved every bit of hair off of her. I'd been far more thorough than I'd needed to be, but we'd needed the moment, the break from the fear.

"Stop thinking about the bad times," she signs to me, "they're over."

"I was thinking," I catch the tear on my cheek far too late, "about the good times."

"These are the good times, Lover," she signs to me, "unless you let my food get cold. Then I'll make them very bad."

"Oh?" I lean in, my teeth peeking out of my smile like a snarl, "you'll punish me, will you? Think you can?"

"No," she backs down so easily, "but I'll be upset."

"That," I smile more cheerfully, "I absolutely forbid. I'd have to punish myself."

I return my attention to the food, and the now.

Once finished, Abeba collects the dishes. When I reach out for her ass she slaps my hand away and wags her finger. I'm speechless, until she places the tray of macaroons on the table. Her lips move in, kissing me, her hand on my shoulder to keep me from rising up into the kiss. I am more than satisfied with dinner. Now I'm hungry for something else, and she knows it. When those soft, full lips, move back from my own they're smiling. Her hand rises into the gap, not signing just leading, leading to the plate. She picks up one of the treats and brings it to my mouth. It's soft, chewy, decadent. Dark chocolate and coconut textures roll around on my tongue. She watches my eyes close as I indulge her. It truly is delicious.

"I'll have two," I tell her, when my eyes open again, "and you will go upstairs while I savor them. The bed has been prepared, you'll need to use your teeth for the last cuff but, don't worry. I'll tighten them."

Her eyes widen. We often take turns asking the other to stay out of the bedroom while we prepare some surprise or another. Today was my turn. Our bedroom is full of delights. A custom built four post bed with bondage rings built into its corners. A throne and play area beside the closet. We've bound other women to the posts so we could fall asleep watching them. We've had orgies with our friends. There are a million devilish delights waiting in that room, and Abeba never knows what to expect. I pour a glass of milk and shove her towards the door. She's timid as she heads upstairs. The macaroons really are good. I savor each bite as I listen to her footsteps. Tonight, I've done nothing too obvious in the bedroom. I've simply fit the bed with restraints connected to each post. Cuffs for her ankles and wrists. We have a St. Andrew's cross up there, but I want her more comfortable tonight. God help her if she falls asleep though.

The second macaroon is no more than crumbs as I wrap the rest. Poor Flower has been quiet upstairs for some time. I prance my way slowly, careful not to make too much noise. When I open the door, I see my favorite sight. Abeba on the bed, limbs spread and body twitching with need. I slide my way into the room, prancing over. One by one, I check and tighten the straps. The ankles, she did well, the wrists need to be tightened. Now, the only way to ask me for anything, will be to use her voice. Once she's trapped, I fluff her pillow. She needs to have her head up to watch me. I begin by slowly pulling off my top before leaning against the bed post and making a show of undoing the fastens on my skirt. I open it away from her, just one more second of teasing until I'm in nothing but my boots. Abeba's eyes follow me as I prance around the bed.

"I know you wanted candy and pink," I tell her, "and I know just the thing." Abeba's eyes keep following as I prance over to our closet. Filled with toys, she can only moan with expectation as my fingers dance along whips, paddles and various other implements of pain and pleasure. Finally, I settle on something pink. Abeba's condition makes most vibrators less effective. They can get the job done, with patience, but there are faster ways. A G-spot vibe, in particular. Pink and curved, thicker than many. I tease my hands around its soft, velvety cover, feeling the powerful motors within. When I glance at Abeba, I see her eyes widen. I must have that predatory smile again, the one that lets her know she's in trouble.

"Do you love me?" I ask her, she nods. "Say it, Flower." She shakes her head. When Abeba says "I love you" it comes out more like, "I of you" and makes her voice sound comically deep. She's embarrassed by it. Abeba is not permitted to dislike any part of herself in my presence. "No?" I say, as I sit on the edge of the bed, "I guess you don't love me then." An indignant noise, a toss of the head. "I know," my voice cracks as I speak, "but I love the sound and I am going to hear it. In fact," I turn, crawling my way up her body to kiss her, "that'll be your safe word for the rest of the night."

My kisses work down her body to the chain of the clamps, she tastes better than any of the food we've eaten. I take the chain in my teeth and sit up, tugging as her moans turn into yelps. The clamps bite, pull and finally pop off but Abeba does not speak. I sigh, undoing her bra and tossing it aside before sliding lower. Her thong is soaked, the panties bunching between her thighs, the strings pulling tight. I look up at her, smiling as she realizes that these are yet another pair to toss out. Don't worry, I only nip her a few times as I chew the straps, one-by-one. I rise again, her thong in my teeth as I toss it aside, her body exposed and helpless under me as I twirl the vibrator in my hand. Her soft lips press tightly as she meets my eye. So be it, I have ways of making her talk.

Abeba's hips rise and fall, desperate for penetration as I tease her body. I know where she's sensitive, a friend of ours had even discovered that the scar replacing her clit could still bring her some pleasure. I use all of my knowledge, my expert understanding of her body. She doesn't speak, however, not a word...save for turning her wrist to flip me off. When the vibe slides into her, she shifts, stills. There's a moment of adjustment as I work the curve and press it up into the spongy tissue behind where her clit used to be. It's just the body of the vibrator at first. I brush my fingers across the power button, but I don't start it yet.

"You will cook me dinner, wear skimpy lingerie, let me torment you. You will even bless me with that one little word, but you won't say what I long to hear." I move the vibe inside of her, letting her feel me penetrating her. "Yes," I say, reading her expression, "I know why you don't want to, and you know why I do want it. We know each other so well, Flower. That says it all right there, doesn't it?" She smiles at me, "but you're still going to say it. Because I want to hear it," my smile turns colder, "and because I won't stop until you do."

The vibrator comes alive so easily. Abeba doesn't complain. She winces, gasps, then starts to moan as I position it. I work it inside of her, one hand then the other, bringing her to orgasm, letting her rest a moment, then starting again. Some may think that that isn't cruel at all. Those people are used to stopping at two, maybe three climaxes. Each time she cums, the muscles of her body tire, the sensations build higher before pushing her over the next edge. Each time it's more intense. By the fifth, I have to start fucking her with the vibe. By the eighth, I have to toy with her butt a little as well. By the tenth it takes her nipples, butt and pussy. Not easy, juggling all of her erogenous zones, but worth it. She's squirting now, trying to pull her hips away from the toy, making noises with her mouth. I know, if she could speak, she'd be pleading with me for mercy. She'd offer to do anything I wanted, if I'd only give her a respite. Some women even claim that they can't cum anymore, that they've reached their limits and that their bodies are broken. The next orgasm, after they've said that, tends to make them scream. Abeba is ready to scream. I focus, working her body this way and that. There's another orgasm building, and I genuinely wonder if she'll be able to take it. Her pussy is red and hot, her muscles are trembling.

"Sop," she pleads, "sop, sop, sop."

"Say what I want to hear," I turn down the intensity of the vibe lest it numb her.

"I of you Yane," she says at last.

My heart skips a beat. My hands fall to my side and her body pushes the vibe away. I stare at her, she back at me. My vision blurs with tears as she gasps. Slowly, methodically, I release the restraints. She pulls away, balling up. I reach out, taking her hand, pulling her into my arms. I kiss her head, her lips. Cradling her in my arms and rocking, fighting tears. Eventually, she pushes me back. My heart starts to pound, an electric shock of fear goes through my tongue. For the millionth time, this week alone, she makes me worry that I've taken things too far. Her expression is inscrutable at first, then it melts into a smile.

"You know I hate it when you make me do that," she signs.

"You know I love it when you do it," I say.

"Now what?" She asks.

"Now I hold you in my arms all night, silly." I try to pull her to me but her hand presses firmly on my shoulder.

"No." She stabs the air firmly. "No cuddles. Not yet."

"Why not?" I ask, as she stretches her arms and cracks her neck.

"Because," she takes my arm and pulls me to my side, rolling me onto my back as she brings a wrist cuff over, "now it's payback time."

"I should have gone for the candies and pink," I giggle.

"And roses," she taps my nose, "every girl wants roses."

"I could have run them across your body," I sigh.

"There's always next year." She cuffs the other hand then moves to my ankles.

"No," I whisper to myself, as she goes to the closet for a fresh toy, "next year a ring."

The Sea of Love

A Gazore Series

Short Story

by

Will Hallewell

Chapter 1

The sea out before us, the horizon there,
I watch as the sun bakes the sky.
And now, as I watch the 'ol island fade on,
I just want to sit down and cry.

Just where was my thinking, back there on that ship
that brought us back home just today?
Was my mind confused, or 'twas something else then
like pirates that caused me to sway?

I look at him there, at the helm, in the front of
our boat, rather small in its way.
And nothing to do except speak my true mind,
I open my mouth and I say...

"Jack, my dear Jack," though my speech is not loud, it
is filled with the joy of his name.
He turns and he looks and he gives me a smile,
and suddenly, I'm not the same.

His eyes are like diamonds, well one of them is.
His beard white, his hair quite a mess.
What I saw in him sometimes I don't know, but
I do know that he is the best.

He sighs as he looks at me, and then I sigh back.

Be My Valentine

"My love," are his words right and fair.
"I do love the sea and the freedom it brings,
but I shouldn't have left you there.

"Alone on the island."

"Oh, but I wasn't alone," I replied as I looked away and out over the vastness of the sea. My voice choked up then and I tried to continue, memories flooding into my brain. Memories of days, months... years past. Happy, very happy, days. "I had friends, my love," I reached out my hand to squeeze his, and God love him, he reached out too. With a tear in my eye, I said, "Lots of friends, generations of friends." And then I sighed and offered up a sad smile, a smile I hoped he didn't recognize the pain in. "And now I have you."

When Jack crossed the small boat and held out his hand to me, I touched it and my heart began to beat wildly. I could feel my insides melt as if they were ice cream left out in the sun or the hands of Chicalito, and I realized that I truly do love this man. I love his wildness and his adventure. I love the way his hair is scattered all over his head like a bird's nest. I even love the whiteness of his beard.

It wasn't always like that, but time will do that to you. Time will eventually, in its slow journey, take the darkest of hair and make it white. It will take the smoothest of skin and make it wrinkled. It will make the strongest of bones, weak. Yet, it can't touch your

spirit.   Oh, it can if you allow it, but don't allow
it. Always keep the child inside.

The child inside, oh yes, the young child inside,
it's there from the start of our lives.
And though we grow old, the young child it stays strong.
Quite strong 'til the day that we die.

"You do at that," Jack held fast to my hand as he
answered my vow of love, and took in our
surroundings. I recognized that young sense of awe in
his eyes that he had from the start of our time together,
and following his gaze, I noticed that the island Gazore
was only a speck behind us. On the other side of the
boat, the vastness of the sea stretched out in front of us,
and we both took in its majesty and its azure-
colored beauty. The sun was dropping down, down,
down into the horizon as if being put away neatly for
the night, and I was quickly reminded of those
wonderful Winter Solstices we had at our home, the
children so carefully taking ornaments from the chest
and placing them on the tree. The sun would soon rise
again, just like those ornaments, and be placed neatly in
the sky once more.

Catching a glimpse of the island we left then,
I saw it just wither and fade.
My memories stirred of the time and the place,
the faces and all that was made.

The children I taught, generations of them,
the parents and their young ones too.
The love that we shared in that small little house
was something that I'd prolly rue.

But then there was Jack and the time in the past
when we were young, holding our hands.
We loved and we laughed with our wild youthfulness.
And we did what no one else can...

I mean, could. We did what no one else could.

We built that small hut with our own very hands.
Jack hammered and sawed. So did I.
And when it was done and the children all came,
Jack's duty was done. That poor guy.

I have to admit that in my loneliness on that island I often blamed him for what happened. I often blamed him for leaving me alone, in our house. I blamed him for all of the things that ever went wrong, but... after Ruby left, what else was there to do?

Jack had done his work, building our house, raising our daughter, but this was before the toys. Long before the toys. Had he known about the toys, he might have stayed on. Working at the factory might have been enough adventure to keep him home, taking into account the way those crazy toys worked. Still, who can say? Jack was more adventurous than he was a factory worker. His mind was full of ideas and adventures that I could never comprehend. And the sea? The sea called out to him it's siren song, and...

"I'm starting to chill," I said then to my Jack.
And as he does, he was prepared.
A box at the base of the helm held a throw
and on my back, it was put there.

"Tank you," I said as the sun finally set down.
The dusk wound right into my eyes.
And as my lids drooped, I heard Jack whisper out,
"Ah, Ruby," and softly he cried.

"Ruby, Ruby, Ruby," his voice echoed into my mind as I drifted away, the gentle motion of the boat rocking me ever so slowly into slumber.

Chapter 2

Dreamland

Her hair was like wheat, tousled upon her head.
She looked like her dad, smile and all.
And when she called "Mama" and "Papa" to us,
we ran with the swiftest footfall.

She was born with such love, that sweet child of mine.
And never was such love so great.
We loved from the start, and then to the end,
and never too little too late.

For me, that's the moment that I started teaching.
When Ruby was young and was fair.
Her friends would come over to our little hut,
and I would teach them and her there.

Their kind eager faces all looked up at me,
then parents of other kids come.
Their kids came along and learned all the things that
the school wasn't teaching to them.

We learned of the Kerr and we learned of the Grale.
We learned of the island so fair.
The forests and animals that it held true.
We learned of the birds of the air.

We learned of the sea and the fish of the deeps.
We learned of da sun and da moon.
The reading and writing I left to the schools.
I taught kids the ways of the loon.

All of this, it seemed was to give Ruby what
the classes were not giving them.
I sure didn't mean then for it to grow up
and for other things then to stem.

But it did.

Our Ruby was always the adventurous one. Just like her best friend, Betty Rae, Ruby had a heart for adventure. We would often find the two of them, deep into the forest or down by the sea, her and Betty Rae playing like two young girls should play. With Ruby, there was a multitude of questions. Every day there was a new discovery. Every day there was a new set of questions. I began to base my lessons with the children on her adventures because I thought that the kids would like them. Little did I know that what I was teaching them was something that eventually would be frowned on by the council.

They didn't like adventure that much, the council. Oh sure, they liked what I was teaching the children, stretching their imaginations, but when it came time for the kids to really go out and explore on their own, they weren't that agreeable. Rules and regulations were put into place to keep the Islanders on the island, but as Ruby and Betty Ray grew older, it became harder and harder to keep them in place.

When Betty Ray finally left and headed for the mainland where she met that intolerable Mo Chalmers, Ruby was heartbroken. Her sense of adventure seemed to increase then, and she became a target for the council.

I tried to intercede, to keep her quiet, to keep her on the island and behaving, but keeping Ruby down became something like trying to tame a wild pony on the mainland. It just wasn't possible.

She wanted to travel like her best friend did.
She wanted to sail the seas.
And when she requested to leave our fair land,
her requests became silenced pleas.

"Mama," she'd shout to me night after night then.
I couldn't accept all her pain.
I tried to talk reason, I tried to calm down
her anger - I could not sustain.

"There's more to the world than just this small island,"
She'd yell as we stood by the sea.
"I know that my love, but just what can I do?
I think that with them I agree."

And that was the point where we started to fail her.
Her anger at me was quite strong.
And like Betty Rae, my small little tike was
no longer, quite actually, young.

"I'm going with dad," she cried out to me then.
"The next time that he goes away."
Then stormed away from me, gone now for years.
Not giving me a chance to say...

Goodbye.

That you must see, is why I like Gemina.
Her spirit is wild, it is free.
My only hope is that I didn't tie her down.
I don't want her to be like me.

I do in some sense, in the sense that she teaches.
I do in the sense that she loves.
I do in the sense that she's good with the children,
and teaches them of turtle doves...

And kerr and grale.

Still, I want her to be free to do what she likes. I
want her and Rock-O to raise a family of their own and
grow and have wonderful lives. I want her to make the
island her home as I did, but I want her to keep her sense

of adventure as well. And I think that she can. I
think that she can be more than me. Better than me.

> *I feel the waves gently rock me awake now,*
> *my eyes slowly starting to see.*
> *I blink rather hard and I look at the helm*
> *just in time to see Jack look at me.*

> *"My love," he just whispers in my waiting ears.*
> *"I heard you cry out her dear name."*
> *I saddened a bit. My lips they turned down and*
> *I nodded a bit in my shame.*

> *"Would you like to go where I left her," he asked.*
> *And then my soul leaped in my chest.*
> *I tried to fight back all the tears that welled up,*
> *but couldn't and so I cried, "Yes!"*

> *"Yes!"*
> *"Yes!"*

Jack smiled and quickly returned to the helm where
he gave the boat a sharp turn to the right. And then it
occurred to me, something I'd never thought of before
in all my time on the island.

> *In all his adventures out there on the sea,*
> *in all of the time he was gone,*
> *he had to have seen her. He had to know where*

and what my dear Ruby had done.

Chapter 3

Patmos Island

In his enthusiasm, Jack began to ramble...

"The islands around our great island, Gazore,
they number four, no not just three.
Esperanza, Patmos, Amor, Tempesta.
Their names all have meaning, you see.

"Hope, Peace and Love, and then sadly the Tempest.
I guess there is always one bad.
I wish that there wasn't, but what can you do?
You can't have happy without sad.

"You cannot have good without the word evil.
You can't have love without some hate.
You can't have..." and then I stopped that 'ol Jack quick.
"Go faster, it's getting quite late."

I couldn't see his face, for the dusk had gone to dark, and all that showed were some outlines, but I knew Jack well enough to know what his expression was: never actually angry, just a playful expression of anger. I smiled in the darkness and looked around at the surrounding blackened sky, and I could almost hear Jack's smile form on his face.

"Hmm," he offered to me and I chuckled.

"You know how you get, husband of mine," I offered up softly, the wind carrying my words to him.

"You talk with your hands and you talk with your eyes.
Your words they go round and around.
Why can't you just tell me the islands are four?
And here are their names. That's quite sound."

Then there was some silence and I thought that I
had given Jack a quick little rile.
But words crossed my ears, coming back on that wind
and all I could do then was smile.

"You need to how everything comes together.
You cannot have A without B."
"You can," I replied, with a smile back at him,
"but I love that you give it to me.

"Still, sometimes, less is more."

I kind of chuckled then, not sure if Jack heard it, but when a long silence ensued (ensued means began), I wondered if maybe I really had made him mad. I tried to change the subject quickly, but he was already one step ahead of me. He recognized the need to move things along, and he did without any more needless discussion.

"Ruby lives on the island, Patmos. We'll be there soon."

I was beginning to drift off to sleep with the setting of the sun, but now at the mention of her name again my heart began to flutter and I awoke with a renewed sense of energy. "How long," I asked softly, counting on the wind to carry my words once more, not knowing how Jack might know such things in the darkness, let alone in the day. He answered me without even having to say the words that I was thinking.

> *"By the stars in the sky, we travel the night.*
> *They guide us, by sun in the day.*
> *And as we press on, the whole universe lit,*
> *I'd say we aren't too far away.*
>
> *"Perhaps we are five, maybe ten minutes more.*
> *I'd say we are fifteen at tops.*
> *Still, I won't go on, I won't ramble about.*
> *We'll get there when we fin'ly stop."*

I shook my head. He was trying to get to me, to pay me back for complaining about his stories when a few words would do, but I wasn't going to put up with his self-pity. "Jack," I started to scold him, but then was silenced as the boat lurched to a sudden halt, almost tossing me onto the shoreline that was invisible, somewhere in front of us, hidden by the black veil of darkness.

"Aha," Jack announced. "Or maybe, less than five minutes." He laughed and I could hear him getting out of the boat and splashing in the water. I pulled the throw that Jack had given me tighter around my shoulders and started to shift in my seat as he tugged us up on what must be the sand. He anchored the little boat, but then his words stopped me.

"Wait here," he announced as he climbed right back in.
"Soon, moonlight will aid in our sight."
And as we sat still, I then marveled at him.
"I don't doubt that you might be right."

I looked at the sky, the two dippers above,
North Star and Cassiopeia.
And then as I wondered at this large display,
Jack spoke to me, "I can see ya!"

Sure enough, then, his old features appeared,
His beard and his patch on his eye.
I smiled as I touched his roughened old face then.
"You sure are a handsome old guy."

From over my shoulder, just there on my left,
moon rose from the depths of the sea.
Jack's hand was outstretched and he helped me right up.
"Come, my love. Just follow me."

I stepped from the boat, the sand wet from the sea.

And I thought of Island, Gazore.
A pang in my heart ached to be there again,
but here there was something much more.

Here, there was Ruby.

"Hold tight to my hand, my love. We have to make this trip by memory, but it's not a long trip. I'll get us to shelter and we can hunker down for the night."

"Shelter," I asked, still a bit in disbelief, but trusting in the knowledge that Jack was way more of an adventurer than I had ever been. We trudged on through the sand, up toward some trees I could make out the outline of, and I asked, "are we going in there?"

Jack shushed me then. "Shh. I know where we are. It's not far,"

"Maybe five or ten minutes," I asked with a playful coyness to my voice.

Jack laughed back at me then, his voice soft as we became surrounded by the trees. "Maybe less."

We walked and we trod, we walked and we trod then,
the minutes passed by, way past ten.
"Or maybe more," I spoke out in the darkness,
Jack snorted to me, "Way past ten."

And then we stopped quick. A light rustle ensued
(ensued means that it had begun).
And as I stepped forward, I felt a light breeze.

A door closed behind; its song sung.

"What is this place," I then asked in the darkness,
The only light that of the moon.
And with a soft strike of a match on a book,
A candle was lit in the gloom.

"This is my home away from home," Jack's reply came to me with a soft kiss on the cheek.

I think it was then that I realized just how much I had missed this man when he had been out traveling the seas; and how much of life I had missed out on.

"There's a cot up against the wall," Jack motioned to the bed. And as I looked around, I took in as much as I could see of his place. Still, the cot sounded inviting so I went there and sat, and looked around, and swiftly gave into the tendrils of sleep that called my name.

"I'll see it in the morning," I whispered.

"You'll see it all in the morning," Jack replied as he slid onto the cot next to me the best that he could, his arm wrapped around me, holding me securely.

"I love you," was the last thing I remember telling him that night, and "I love you," was the last thing I remember hearing back.

Chapter 4

Flora and Jackie

A scream woke me up and I sat in a fright!
A bird of some kind screamed quite loud.
"Now you settle down," Jack climbed right over me.
And to the door, he strode quite proud.

The sun had returned, as the great sun will do,
and Jack, he then opened the door.
A rather large bird with his feathers all wild,
Strode in on two legs, "This is Flor."

"Well, her name is really Flora, but we shortened it to Flor because we thought she needed a nickname."

"Subtracting one letter is not a nickname," I replied in disbelief, sliding up to a sitting position on the cot.

"Well, Ruby and I do all sorts of silly things," Jack started, but then stopped because he realized what he was saying, and didn't want to hurt my feelings. He crossed over to me and sat down.

"I know you haven't seen her for quite a while and I have, but now…," Flora squawked again as Jack kissed my forehead and headed over to where there was a washbasin sitting on a cabinet. He opened the cabinet, scooped out some kind of food into a bowl, and set it down on the ground. He returned to me as Flora ran to the food, her wings flapping comically hard. "You will."

His eyes were quite warm, full of promise right then,
and mine became filled with some tears.
I wiped at my cheeks and I took a deep breath.
I hoped I could fight through my fears.

Of seeing my daughter again.

"The things she must think of me, never being around for her," I couldn't help it, the tears just came and I covered my face to hide them. I felt horrible for being so selfish back then, but...

What of the kids that I taught all those years there,
back on the island Gazore?
Didn't I matter in their tiny lives, or
did they think of me nothing more

than just a kind woman who babysat them
and scolded when they acted bad?
"I'm having a bit of confusion right now,"
I said. "The whole thing makes me sad."

Then Jack, in his Jack sort of way, gently took my hands away from my face and held them. I looked up and met his eyes which were kind and soft and melted my fears away. Behind him, Flora was looking at me with huge blue eyes, her head cocked slightly to the right as if assessing my every move, and I began to laugh. And I mean laugh hard.

At first, Jack didn't know what to think, I could tell by the way he narrowed his eyes at me, his soft and reassuring words erased from his lips, but then he looked over his shoulder and laughed just as hard.

"Oh, ya silly bird," he muttered and turned to wave the bird forward. "C'mon, now. She's just as gentle as you, she's not going to harm ya. Go over and see for yourself."

Flora followed his gesturing, and then took one hesitant step toward me. I wiped the remaining tears away and bent down with inviting arms out her way. "It's okay, Flora. I won't hurt you. I'm Mama Eche…"

And then, one more time, I got caught on my words.
To Jack, I had once been Raeni.
The word it meant, Queen, but that was now gone.
Mama Eche meant much more to me.

I was once a teacher, not sitter of kids.
I molded and tended those hearts.
But, I had retired, and now here I was.
In a hut with a brand-new start.

I leaned down and held out my hands with confidence now. "C'mon, Flora. I won't hurt you. I'm Raeni." And Flora slowly, and with growing confidence, accentuated with each new step, made her way toward me. I felt overjoyed as I reached out and petted her and she softly relaxed under my aged hands. I felt as if I were shedding my skin, becoming who I had left behind for all of those years. I was beginning to feel alive and new and happy, confident in my future as my past self, but then this happened…

As I petted the bird, eyes facing the door,
I saw it swing open right there.
A boy entered in like a gust of the wind,
and shouted to Jack, "Mi, Grandpere!"

I knew from that instant, that Raeni and Mama Eche were about to be snuffed out and replaced, but replaced by… whom?

"Ah, Jackie," Jack laughed as he ran to the lad.
His arms were all open quite wide.
They hugged a long time and I felt rather odd,
when the boy looked at me and cried,

"Who dat?"

"I was aghast at two things in my mind then:
his pointing and language he used.

Be My Valentine

The language was dismal, just terribly bad, and
the pointing? Just nasty and rude.

Jack turned then to me and he held out his arm.
"That, little Jackie's your Grandmere."
The boy's eyes grew narrow cause he had his doubts.
He clutched Jack's hand with a small scare.

"Grandmere," Jackie looked up at Jack, still confused, and Jack tried his best to help him along, even though I had my doubts that he was going to catch on. He bent down to the lad's side, and looked at his face and then mine.

"Grandpere," He pointed at his own chest, then pointed at me (again, rude, but I guess he had to make himself clear). "Grandmere."

The boy's eyes stayed wide, his 'ol mouth hung agape.
He couldn't get through this trauma
of knowing my name and relationship. Then,
he turned on a dime and said, "Mama!"

He started to tug on the hand of 'ol Jack
and I think in that moment there,
I finally grasped what I had been hearing.
Jack, my husband, was a Grandpere…

And I was a Grandmere…

And Ruby was Mama…

And Jackie… Jackie was my grandson!

I jumped to my feet at the cries from my husband to hurry along, and with a smile on my face and delight in my heart I followed. I followed my grandson and his Grandpere, as we ran onto a path, deeper into the woods toward who knew where.

As we ran, my mind whirred in circles. I studied Jackie as his little feet carried him like the wind, Jack trying to keep up, and I surmised that he must have been around five years old. His skin was the typical green color of islanders that I had known on the island Gazore, and his hair was as wild as… well, as his mother's. This made me smile. If Ruby's child was going to have a trait that would stand out, it would be his hair.

Jackie stopped and then turned to me, his eyes dark.
"You hurry, Grandmere. You come on."
I chuckled and laughed, a small combination,
And replied, "I'm on my way, son."

Chapter 5

Oss-Oss and Grumby and Mama

And so I sped up and I ran and I ran.
The forest, it grew rather dense.
Then, inside a clearing, I saw the first signs
of the islanders. There was a fence.

I stopped my feet running and Jackie called out,
"Grandmere, don't stop coming."
But I couldn't help it, not me not at all.
What I saw was visibly stunning.

Behind that long fence, and I mean very long,
were those same birds, just like Flora.
I tilted my head, just like that same bird, and
I shouted out, "There are some more... a."

And then, of course, I was embarrassed. I had the name Flora so locked in my mind, that I rhymed it just like Doug and Ellie had done in our last adventure. The only difference was that here there was no G.O.T. here. At least I hoped not!!

Jackie brought me back by grabbing my hand that had been hanging at my side. His touch was so electric to me that I felt my heart melt inside my chest as if the charge were melting and transforming me from the inside out. "Dat's Oss-Oss, Grandmere," he looked over the fence, his other hand pointing at the large birds inside the fence.

"Oss-Oss," I asked, confirming what he had said, and older Jack finally joined us.

"Oss-Oss," he confirmed my confirmation, leaning against the fence with his arms on the top rail. He studied the birds for a few contemplative seconds before turning to me with a smile. "Oss-Oss are used in Grumby games. The players ride them."

> I nodded as if I knew what he had meant,
> but Oss-Oss and Grumby were new.
> "I'm kind of confused," I admitted to them.
> "What do those people there do?"

Inside the fence there were people with the Oss-Oss, male and female islanders so it seemed, and they were dressed in some kind of uniform. Not a uniform like a military uniform, but like a sporting uniform. They were swiftly mounting and dismounting the Oss-Oss, sometimes standing still and other times while at a full gallop. Occasionally, they would bend over to one side in full gallop, as if reaching for something on the ground. Then they would ride and dismount, not waiting one second for the birds to stop running.

> "They're training," Jack said as he studied my face.

288

"For Grumby," I asked like I knew.
"Exactly," Jack said in a kind of surprise.
"I didn't think you knew, whoo-hoo!"

I have to admit that I was embarrassed a bit, but in my defense, I had never seen animals like the Oss-Oss. The only animals we have on Island Gazore are the birds of the air. And no one ever trains them. "Are these the only animals on the island? We don't have anything like this…"

"I know," replied Jack, then he grabbed Jackie's hand
and started to lead him away.
"There's more," he said as went up the path,
and I had to run, not sashay.

"Now where are we going," I panted and huffed.
A hill was right there before us.
"Just over the hill, a small crest in the land,
and then you'll see what's all the fuss."

All the fuss? I didn't get it. What I did get, however, was two things:

I was an old lady. Too old for running up hills.
When Jackie came back to me, took my hand
and cried out, "C'mon, Grandmere, let's go!" it didn't
matter.

I ran like the wind.

And as we ran on, the hill higher and higher,
I panted and wheezed in my chest.
That didn't stop me. No how, no, not ever.
For suddenly, this was the best.

This was the best part of my life. The Islanders on Gazore were melting away with each step. Remi, Aida, Barnes, Noble, Gemina, Rock-O, Vern, Rose, Doug and Elly, Chicalito… all of the craziest things that had gone on before, melting away like my insides when Jackie spoke to me, touched my hand.

The hill it went on and on, no end in sight.
Then finally, we reached the top.
We stopped for a breath and my jaw dropped open.
The forest was gone with our stop.
And what lay ahead was amazing to me.
A circle of huts 'round a field.
And not just a field of a minuscule size,
but a field of a glorious yield.

The huts and the field were all hidden away
by some plants standing eight feet tall.
The stalks of these plants each held one ear of corn,
but corn on Gazore didn't fall.

I'd heard of it, sure, but I never did see

such a plant, such a field as this.
"C'mon, Raeni," Jack came to take up my hand
and gave me a small, perfect kiss.

"Wait until you see what waits for you down on the pitch," Jack instructed and Jackie became as excited as a five-year-old can get. He began to jump up and down and spin himself in circles, shouting two words over and over again, "Grumby" and "Mama!"

My heart, it was melting, but not from the touch
of a little boy, I just met.
Instead, I was here, just a step or two more
from the daughter, I hadn't set…

…eyes on in years.

Chapter 6

Finally, Ruby

The pitch, it was long and was marked with white lines.
A middle and then the two ends.
Two U shaped contraptions stood tall at each side,
just straight up, there was no U bend.

On each end below the U, there was a line,
much wider there than all the rest.
And as I stared out at the empty green field,
Jack came up and said, "It's the best."

"You see, there's a ball and the players and teams.
And the team with the ball tries to score."
He pointed right down to the U-shaped contraption,
And then he went on. "Still, there's more.

"You see those tall trees on the side of the pitch?
They hang right out over the field.
Well, Swingers swing there from the ropes that hang up
in the branches. They are a shield."

Ropes? I hadn't even noticed the ropes until he mentioned them, figuring that they must have blended in with the tree branches so well that my mind just turned them into part of the tree. Still, here they were, and now, here came some islanders who went to the ropes and climbed them with expert dexterity. Crowd noise increased and Jackie became excited, starting to run down the hill toward the pitch, his young legs carrying him swiftly, and his arms flailing wildly. "C'mon, Grandpere, Grandmere! It's time. Game on!"

"We'd better go," Jack smiled as he took my hand. "I'll tell you more when we get there."

We got there right quick on the wind of that boy,
and he started to scan the pitch.
Then in a parade, all the Oss-Oss were led.
A horn somewhere above made me twitch.

I looked all around and the players all came.
Some dressed well in brown, some in red.
Then Jackie jumped up and down over again.
"Mama," he exclaimed what I dread.

I didn't need Jack to point my way to her.
I'd know her in any old time.
A woman came out, dressed in brown uniform,
but her red hair told me, that's mine.

"She's a forward," Jack said, but his words were a bit lost to me, or maybe I became lost at seeing Ruby again after so long. He rambled, and only later, as the game progressed, did I understand what he was telling me.

> "The Oss-Oss, they carry the riders like her
> down the field. It goes rather fast.
> The swingers, they try to stop them right there, while
> the Oss-Oss, they try to get past."

My daughter, Ruby is an Oss-Oss rider in a Grumby game? She has a son? What has happened to my world? Where was I all of these years, teaching and molding young minds, missing...

> "And when they get past, then the blockers are there.
> Just big guys to knock them right down.
> They sometimes succeed, but yet mostly they don't.
> They're too big. They just go around."

My legs grew weak and I clasped onto Jack's arm for support. I had missed my daughter's entire life. How was she ever going to forgive...

> "And then there's the sneaker," Jack continued on.
> "He hides behind blockers and such.
> He's only a kid, but a talented one.
> And what he does? Well, it is much.

> "He hides and he waits, and then when you are close
> to the goal... well, that's when he strikes!

He steals the ball quick and then makes his escape.
To catch him, you'd have to be like..."

He nodded his way toward the pitch and his daughter...

"Ruby."

A wild chant rose from the crowd, calling my daughter's name over and over again as she crossed the pitch and waited at midfield. "Ru-by! Ru-by!" Even Jackie and Jack got into the chant themselves, Jack calling my daughter's name, and her boy calling, "Ma-Ma! Ma-Ma!"

I have to admit, I got caught up in the excitement and the crowd's roar, and I joined in, "Ru-by, Ru-by!"

Another player joined Ruby at midfield, shook her hand with a cordial smile, then a woman islander in striped shirt brought out the ball. "Referee," Jack informed me. She raised it high above her head, Ruby and the other woman placed their hands on each other's shoulders, then bent down so their heads were touching. The referee placed the ball on the ground between them, blew a whistle, and then the play began.

I had never seen such a thing as I saw
when Ruby tossed that girl aside.
She grabbed up the ball, headed straight for an Oss,
jumped on, and then started to glide.

For their part, the swingers, they all missed their mark.
Not ready for something so quick.
I sure didn't want to see them strike my girl.
To quote Elly, that would be, "Ick."

Some forwards came then, some on foot and some Oss,
but their attempts to stop her failed.
She got to the line and then swiftly was off.
The blockers did not want to yield.

They stepped to their left then they stepped to their right.
Then, Ruby, she did a spin turn.
She got 'round the blockers but then lost the ball.
A sneaker did what sneakers learn.

This one was a girl, maybe same age as Aida,
and this girl could run really fast.
She flew down the field, right there through the swingers,
then she sadly made a bad pass.

I hadn't been watching, my own daughter there,
as she rode an Oss-Oss insane.
She stole that bad pass from the air like a fiend,
and took off toward goal once again.

This time she had help, as another girl there
rode beside her taking her pass.
And then as the swingers attacked from the sky,
Ruby, she did surely surpass...

...everyone's expectations.

It all went too quick for me to see how it happened, but she had that ball tucked between her legs as she used the ropes to swing her way across the field, drop to the ground, put it back in her arms, and head back the way she had come. By now, the other girl had dismounted as well and was running toward Ruby where they somehow exchanged the ball, effectively confusing the blockers and sneakers. Both of them ran toward opposite sides of the pitch until the other girl crossed the line and fell to the ground, exhausted.

The team all came then and they all piled right on.
Celebration had surely begun.
And that's when my mind started to go away,
and all of my thoughts came undone.

Where *had* I been all these years? What *had* I been doing?

The last time I had seen this girl who had grown into a woman, she was sailing away with her father. To save myself from going crazy, I had embraced all of the children on the island. I had used them as substitutes for Ruby, my way of justifying letting her go. Now, it felt wrong. It felt as if I had let her down; as if I had let everyone down.

Yet, that wasn't right. I *had* helped a lot of children over the years. I had helped them grow and learn and appreciate life. I *had* helped save the island in some way, hadn't I? When Mo Chalmers took over and those Verns came... I *had* helped. *Hadn't* I? Hadn't I been their source of guidance? Hadn't I been a strong force in their lives?

I was beginning to doubt myself as these thoughts and worries increased, my mind going to a darker place, but then I felt a small hand bring me back into *this* time and place, and I looked down at Jackie who was pulling at me.

"C'mon, Grandmere. We go see Mama."

I tried to stop him from pulling me forward,
my mind became filled with such fright.
But right then it happened and Ruby appeared.
My mind became filled with delight.

A short-lived delight.

She studied my face as she drew ever near.
The game done, all of the drama.
I studied her eyes and I found a weak smile.
In a soft voice, she said, "Mama?"
Jackie called to her, pointing right there at me.
"It's Grandmere," he called my name proud.
Then Ruby did something that stabbed through my heart.
She called to Jackie rather loud.

Be My Valentine

"Jackie, get behind me."

I knew right away that things were not the same.
I started to cry, yes, I did.
"Why are you here," she asked me rather coldly.
And then she picked up her small kid.

And started away.

I briefly remember falling to my knees, but words wouldn't come. Only tears.

Ruby took Jackie away from me, walking in the opposite direction, heading toward the huts, and I lowered my head to the ground. I heard Jack call her name and then step away from me in a quick rush, and I thought to myself the strangest thing...

How will I get home?

When I finally looked up, the three of them stood,
still standing and shouting quite mad.
Then Jack came to me, took my arm, helped me up.
And Ruby quite tired, called out, "Dad."

"She stays far away from me. Me and my son."
But Jack wasn't listening to this.
"It's gonna be fine," he said softly to me.
And then he gave me a small kiss.

On the cheek.

We followed along at a pace rather far,
We finally got to the huts.
She took in her son, not a word to us then,
and I said, "I think I am nuts."

"Jack, she doesn't want me here." I was being reasonable now, finally able to make coherent thoughts, and I put them out there for all to hear. I stopped walking, but Jack's hand never left my arm.

"She's just upset, my love. She didn't know we were coming."

"Still, I thought... hoped... that she might be glad to see me. Instead, she's done what she always did when I made her mad. She's shut me out."

This gave Jack a smile and he shared it with me.
"I ask you to look, I implore."
And then when I followed his gesturing hand,
To the hut, he said, "Open door."

And as I looked, I realized Jack was right. Not bad for a man who claimed to be some kind of pirate, venturing out on who knew what kind of adventures, only to return when I needed him most. Not bad for a father who remained a dad to his daughter and a Grandpere to boot. Not bad for a man who somehow managed to keep his family together, even when we had drifted so far apart. Not bad for a wild-haired husband.

I kissed him lightly on the lips and wiped away the tears. "Open door," I replied to him with a heavy sigh, holding his hand instead of him holding my arm. Together we walked through that open door and into our future, no matter what it would bring.

And oh, what it would bring.

About the Publisher

Kingston Publishing offers an affordable way for you to turn your dream into a reality. We offer every service you will ever need to take an idea and publish a story. We are here to help authors make it in the industry. We want to provide a positive experience that will keep you coming back to us.

Whether you want a traditional publisher who offers all the amenities a publishing company should or an author who prefers to self-publish, but needs additional help - we are here for you.

Now Accepting Manuscripts!
Please send query letter and manuscript to:
submissions@kingstonpublishing.com
Visit our website at www.kingstonpublishing.com

Made in the USA
Middletown, DE
01 February 2022

59784415R00169